SAM CASTLE'S
CIRCUS

WALT DISNEY'S
Toby Tyler

Adapted from the Walt Disney
motion picture TOBY TYLER

Authorized Edition

Told by

DOROTHEA J. SNOW

Illustrated by

BEN FRANKLIN

WHITMAN PUBLISHING COMPANY
RACINE, WISCONSIN

Ever think of joining a circus, lad?"

Toby Tyler could hardly believe his ears! What could *he* do in the wonderful world of the circus?

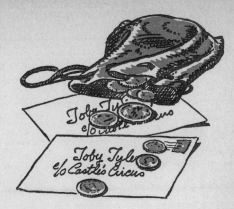

He was soon to find out. Certain that Uncle Daniel and Aunt Olive no longer wanted him, Toby one night entered into the strange, new life.

It was not the life he had expected; the glitter of the big show had a different look from behind the scenes. Working for mean Mr. Tupper at the candy stand was the hardest job Toby had ever known. But there was funny, loving Mr. Stubbs the chimpanzee to bring some happiness into his life. And there were other friends—Ben the strong man, Sam the clown, and Jeanette the beautiful little bareback rider.

Eventually Toby had a chance to become a star in his own right. *Monsieur Toby,* the posters read! Plain Toby Tyler had come a long way.

It was at the height of his glory that Toby made the hardest decision of his life. What it was, why he made it, and what happened then make a thrilling climax to the story of *Toby Tyler.*

CONTENTS

1   NO TICKET!

"Toby! Toby Tyler!"

The querulous voice of the old man sounded across the barnyard and assaulted the ears of the ten-year-old boy standing beside the weather-beaten barn.

A slight grimace flickered across Toby's plain, freckled face. He squinched his eyes shut and hunched his sturdy shoulders in an effort to shut out the unwelcome sound.

"Toby! Toby Tyler!"

Again the voice of Uncle Daniel pierced the reluctant hearing of the redheaded boy. It did no good to try not to hear. Uncle Daniel's voice was one that could be heard a mile away.

Sighing heavily Toby gave a last longing look at the circus poster plastered on the side of the old, faded red barn that stood on his uncle's farm. It was as gaudy as

11

circus posters of its day, around the turn of the century, were apt to be. It read:

COLONEL SAM CASTLE'S
GREAT AMERICAN CIRCUS!

Performance Afternoon and Evening
Rain or Shine!

Featuring
The Mammoth Free and Gratis
Morning Street Parade
Courtesy of Colonel S. Castle!

Below the brightly painted picture of five trapeze artists, flying through the air with the ease of giant birds, were the words:

Guilford   July 2, 1898.

That was today, Toby knew. For weeks he had been keeping his eye on the big calendar that hung in the kitchen of the old farmhouse.

He *had* to see that circus. Work, work, work! Chores, chores, chores! That was all he had known since coming to live with Uncle Daniel and Aunt Olive. Just this once he had to break out of the circle of bleak days.

All the pent-up longing of the past weeks bubbled up in him now and spilled over in a relentless resistance to Uncle Daniel's summons.

Probably just wanted him to fill the wood box, Toby thought. Well, he wasn't going to fill any old wood box today. Not with Colonel Castle's Great American Circus in town! No, sir!

As quick as the flick of a squirrel's tail the boy in patched overalls whisked around the side of the barn, away from the sound of his uncle's voice.

He ran squarely through a small flock of chickens busily pecking at some stray grains of corn that Aunt Olive had strewn there that morning. They set up an indignant squawk at being so rudely disturbed.

"Sh-h-h!" Toby put a finger to his lips, bent over, and sent pleading looks at the angry fowl. "Not so loud!"

The chickens paid no further attention to him and went back to their pecking. Toby sighed with relief and went on, this time careful to look where he was going. Those chickens deserved more respectful consideration, he decided, than he had given them.

He peered around another corner of the barn. There

was the road to town. If only he could get across the yard on this side without being seen. If only he could reach that road. The rest would be easy.

Uncle Daniel's spare, gaunt figure still stood by the back steps of the house, his grizzled head turning slowly as on a pivot, searching, searching.

"If he sees me, I'm a goner," Toby whispered to himself. Hastily he withdrew his head. No use asking for trouble. Likely Uncle Daniel would stand there all afternoon, calling and looking.

If only he could reach the road without being seen! Toby looked around for another means of escape.

That line of berry bushes, the pride and joy of Aunt Olive—it would make a perfect screen to hide his dash to the road.

Using the barn as a shield he made a run for the bushes. Once behind them, he lit out lickity-split for the road. Up and over an old rail fence . . . a dash through dry weeds . . . and he was in a rutted, rocky country lane.

A wild, fierce joy surged through him. He was free! Like a fox let out of his cage for the hunt he lit off down the road as though all the hounds in the world were baying at his heels.

"Toby! Where are you?" Uncle Daniel's voice soon sounded faint and far away.

A half hour later, without ever having slackened his headlong pace, Toby reached the outskirts of the village of Guilford.

The circus was in town all right. And like all circuses of the day, it was busy letting the townfolk of Guilford know it, and at the same time, urging them to come to the first performance that afternoon under the big top.

The parade was on its way down the main street of the village and Toby could hear, from that direction, the rousing notes of the "Double Eagle March!" If he didn't make even more haste he would miss it and have all his trouble for nothing. He drew in a breath fit to burst his lungs, and getting his second wind, he made a faster spurt forward.

Now he could see the crowd of gaily dressed town-folk lining both sides of the main street. He could hear the sounds of delight coming from them. Over their heads he could see the white plumes of some horses nodding up and down. Those must belong to the horses carrying the outriders who came first and told everybody to tie up their horses because the elephants were coming.

If so, he hadn't missed a thing.

He drew up behind the line of people and found they were standing three deep and he couldn't see through them. A flurry of hand clapping, while he was searching for a hole in the crowd through which he could see, made him wonder what he was missing.

Hugging the rear of the crowd he started running in the direction the parade was headed. Somewhere along here . . . ah, there was a tiny space between those two ladies. Triumphantly he squeezed between them.

"Hmph!" sniffed one of them, a tall, thin angular lady with graying hair and a disapproving expression. "The way some folks raise their young'uns, they got no manners at all."

Toby was blissfully unaware of her complaint. Shivering with pure delight he was watching a prancing black horse and its rider coming toward him. Never in all his short life had he seen anything more grand than the handsome, middle-aged man sitting with military bearing astride the shining steed stepping so proudly up the street.

Colonel Sam Castle himself! Toby knew that, because someone had told him the owner of a circus always came first in a parade, except for the outriders who warned the onlookers that the elephants were coming.

On either side of Colonel Castle, and slightly behind him, rode two beautiful ladies. In short flaring skirts of white satin and plumed wide-brimmed hats worn at rakish angles, they sat their horses with such ease that murmurs of admiration went up from the crowd.

"The Double Eagle March" was loud now. The owner of the circus and the beautiful ladies passed so close to Toby that he could have reached out and touched them if he had dared.

Like a big country dinner getting better and better as it worked toward the dessert, the parade kept coming. Atop a gold-and-blue-and-red-scrolled band wagon, pulled by six plumed white horses, sat twelve men in bright blue uniforms playing on horns and trumpets and beating drums that glinted in the bright sunlight. Behind it, their harnesses jingling crisply in time to the music of the band, stepped a troupe of liberty horses.

A loud roar almost sent Toby back into the arms of the sour-faced woman behind him. He looked up. There, just above him but behind the bars of a cage wagon, a tawny lion opened its huge mouth and showed long, sharp white fangs. A sharp-clawed paw was thrust out between the bars. Toby was thankful it was a safe distance from him and the others. Wow, but that lion looked fierce!

With an effort he pulled himself up straight—just in time to see the next wagon full of chattering monkeys, excitedly running about the section of the cage in which they were enclosed or swinging back and forth on the two small trapezes in it. The other half of the cage, Toby noted, held another monkeylike creature considerably larger than the rest.

Just beneath his cage Toby read CHIMPANZEE. Toby shook his head; it looked like a monkey to him. As though reading his thoughts, the chimpanzee stuck his nose through the bars and made a face at him. Toby roared in delight at its antics.

The driver of the wagon turned and looked back to see what had happened; sometimes a monkey got loose in these parades and caused plenty of trouble. Toby got a quick glimpse of a huge man in a striped, knitted shirt that showed off his muscular chest and biceps. He saw, too, the black, bushy brows brought together in a half scowl and was glad that he wasn't a monkey in one of those cages.

An entreating voice, like a magnet, drew his head around.

"Stand back, please! Give way! The elephants are coming!"

But the outriders had said that! Wh . . . ? Toby's eyes went from the clown with the whimsical face and long plaid coat, back along the thick rope to a single line of— dogs, all decked out to look like elephants! Each wore floppy imitation elephant ears and a stuffed cotton "trunk" that curled back and up in an exaggerated fashion and wound around the tail of the one before him.

The crowd howled and so did Toby.

Behind the little "pachyderms" came a real, baby one, disdainfully hanging on to the tail of the dog in front of him and seemingly not at all pleased with this silly foolishness.

Then, suddenly, something swished over Toby's head. The sour-looking lady gave a shriek. Toby looked up. It was the trunk of the little elephant, the real one. And it was greedily reaching into a paper sack held by a man beside her.

Laughing, the man picked out a peanut and gave it to the elephant who took it, curled his trunk under, and snuffed it into his mouth. Toby reached out and cautiously patted the little elephant. How rough his hide felt!

Then Toby looked up and his hand stopped in mid-air. The clown was coming toward him and the little elephant, shaking his finger vigorously and scolding fiercely. Toby thought the clown was scolding, but he couldn't be sure. For no sound came from the clown's mouth though his wide, painted lips were working like anything.

Toby knew then that the clown was just doing this for laughs. He knew it when the white-gloved hand reached over and took the ear of the little elephant and marched him, with exaggerated sternness, down the street.

Everybody laughed, including Toby, though he did hate to lose sight of the clown and his funny little charges.

It was a good thing, though, that the clown took hold of the little elephant when he did, or it would have been ridden over by the towering, colorfully painted wagon that followed. Craning his neck Toby looked up and gasped at the sight of several performers standing in various poses on top of it. All in spangled tights, with bright colored capes swirling about their shapely shoulders, they were a gorgeous sight, like creatures from another

world, a wonderful fairy world.

But then, Toby decided, that was what the circus was— another world, one as far removed from the drab, work- aday world he knew, as the fairies.

Toby sighed. Sometimes he daydreamed of being a fairy prince, riding a handsome charger, and going about the countryside slaying imaginary dragons and rescuing fair damsels in distress. Being a part of a circus would be even better, he reasoned. For the world of the prince was strictly a dreamy never-never land, while the circus was *real*.

Then he was jarred back to his senses. He had leaned so far out to get a good look at the two camels clopping by, carrying a couple of desert sheiks in flowing robes, that he almost fell flat on his face.

There was so much to see! The two ladies were squeezing him like a sponge, but if he went any farther into the street he was liable to become a part of the parade himself!

A fat man who stepped in front of him then appar- ently had no such worries. He was big enough to be a fat man in a circus, Toby thought wryly as he tried desperately to see around him.

Then Toby saw it, not far away. A lamp post! Why hadn't he thought of that before? Quicker than a sneeze he had squeezed his way back through the crowd and was running in its direction. Up the pole he shinnied.

Now he could see everything.

The red ticket wagon rolled past, and then came a group that really made Toby's eyes pop.

These were riders, or equestrians, dressed in dazzling costumes and holding their heads as high and proudly as royal personages which, in the realm of the circus, they are. Best of all, to Toby, among these glamorous folk were a boy and a girl of about his own age!

They were riding side by side. The girl was the prettiest creature Toby had ever laid eyes on, prettier even than the little striped snake he had caught once and scared the living daylights out of Aunt Olive with.

The boy was handsome, too, but Toby saw right away that he carried himself with a nose-in-the-air manner toward the watching crowd. He thought himself better than other folks. Toby could see that and decided he didn't like him.

Toby's eyes and the girl's met for a fleeting second! She waved a tiny, white-gloved hand at him and he almost lost his grip and fell off the pole!

He caught himself just in time to see a cage full of tigers go by. But somehow they seemed, to the dazedly happy Toby, to waver like his own image in the ripples of the creek after he had dropped a pebble into it.

Then his eyes came back into focus. Before them another wagon went by followed by six big, lumbering elephants kept in line by their trainer carrying a pike-and-hook stick. A lady sat on the head of the lead elephant, tiny and dainty and seeming perfectly at home on her bobbing perch.

The wheezing sound of the calliope filled the air as it went by. Dressed in an oilskin coat to protect him from the steam, a man was playing "In the Good Old Summertime."

Toby clung to the post and watched until the last of the parade had gone by, headed toward the circus grounds. The crowd got thinner and thinner until it was practically gone. Then down from the post he slid and went in the direction the calliope had taken.

Around and around the circus grounds he walked and waited for the crowd to come for the afternoon performance. He was so excited that he forgot until later that he was missing his noon meal!

Then the crowd began to drift in and Toby became a part of it on the midway. His mouth half open, he walked slowly along looking up at the banners and streamers on the fronts of the tents, advertising the shows within. On one was a huge picture of a man swallowing a tremendous sword. On another was the likeness of a man juggling sixteen balls in the air at once, and even Toby knew that was impossible.

"Right this way, folks! Get your tickets for the main show!" the man in front of the tent of the sword swallower was crying.

"Get a cane, get a whip! Get a walking stick! Only five cents!" shouted a gravel-voiced lady behind a booth loaded with gimcracks. That was what Uncle Daniel had called the things sold at a circus when he had first seen the poster pasted on his barn. Right then and there Toby had realized it would do no good to ask Uncle Daniel if he could go to see the circus.

"Ice-cold lemonade! Five cents a glass! It's pink! It's cold! It's refreshing!"

Toby's mouth was parched and his stomach was empty. A glass of cold lemonade would hit the spot right now.

"Hurry, hurry, hurry! See the world's most daring high-wire artistes! See the famous liberty horses that performed before the crowned heads of Europe!"

On he went down the midway. The pungent aroma of hot buttered popcorn and roasting peanuts tantalized his nostrils and emphasized the emptiness of his stomach. Those taffy apples that people were munching as they walked along! And the fluffy clouds of spun sugar candy on sticks that other boys and girls were burying their faces in! Toby tried not to notice, but it was hard.

"Get your peanuts! Get your popcorn! Get a taffy apple!" He was passing the stand selling them.

The sights and sounds and smells of the circus enclosed Toby in a happy state of bewilderment. His head turned first one way and then another, like a weathervane in a fickle wind.

One voice was becoming louder as it cried, "Step right this way, folks! Get your tickets at the big red wagon!"

He was nearing the big top. He could hear the band inside striking up a lively air. Now the voice was loud enough to almost drown out the other sounds.

"Hurry now, folks, hurry! The main performance is about to begin! Count your change before you leave the ticket window! Hurry, folks, hurry!"

As though to a magnet Toby was drawn to that urgent sound.

A man with a huge bunch of balloons, of every color of the rainbow, thrust one into his hand.

"Balloon! Toy balloon!" the man wheedled. "All kinds and all colors! Only a penny! One copper penny!"

Toby wanted a balloon. He wanted something he could take home with him that would, every time he looked at it, bring back delightful memories of this day. He fished into his pocket. He brought out the only coin he carried.

Ruefully he looked down at it lying there in the palm of his roughened, brown hand. It was an Indian head penny! Should he spend it?

Nope. He put it back into his pocket and shook his head at the balloon man who went on crying his wares.

Suddenly, from the side, came a shriek.

"My balloon! I want another balloon!"

Toby's head swiveled. There was a small boy, clinging to his father's hand and pointing to a green balloon that, apparently, had gotten away from him and was slowly heading skyward.

Toby grinned and patted the pocket where the penny was. Suppose he had bought a balloon and it had done the same thing! When he spent his penny, he wanted to be sure he got his money's worth.

Toby went a little closer to the main entrance. Close by the ticket taker's rostrum he stopped and stood, wistfully watching others go into the tent.

Finally there was no one left outside but himself and the ticket taker.

"You goin' in?" the ticket taker asked.

Toby sighed sadly.

"Nope," he answered.

Peering past the entrance flap Toby could see that the show had begun. How he wished he could go in! From somewhere close came another voice. "Lemonade! Ice-cold lemonade! Crispy, crunchy, circus peanuts! Get 'em here!"

Harry Tupper, concessionaire, was trying to bring in a few more nickels!

2 FREE PASS

Toby let out a deep sigh. Was there anything worse than being at the entrance of the main tent of a circus, as the show was about to start, and not having a ticket to go in? Nor any money with which to buy one, except one lone Indian head penny?

With a feeling of deep reluctance, Toby turned his back on the entrance of the big top. Valiantly he tried to shut out the sound of the lively tune from within, of the happy murmur of those lucky enough to be waiting for the beginning of the big parade, or spec, of the sight of the performers and animals around the three rings in the center of the tent. Visibly drooping, he started back the way he had come, down the midway.

The midway was empty now, except for the concessionaires behind the counters of their booths, busily tidying up, straightening out their wares, or counting their money.

Toby noticed particularly the stand where lemonade, cotton candy, and peanuts were sold. So that was where that luscious smell had come from! For no reason except the desire for a better whiff Toby walked toward it.

Behind the stand Harry Tupper was busily filling a tray full of taffy apples, striped bags of peanuts, and lemonade glasses. His lean, rather cynical-appearing face was contracted in a frown of concentration, as though he weren't accustomed to doing all this work himself.

Silently Toby stood and watched the man scoop peanuts into bags and twist the upper corners of the sacks into rabbity-looking ears.

Harry looked up and saw the wistful face watching. His own features spread into a wide, affable grin that somehow looked out of place.

"You a buyer or a looker?" he asked, twisting two ears and piling the sack on top of others on the tray.

Carefully Toby rearranged it on the stack from which it looked in danger of falling.

"How many peanuts would you say I could get for a penny?" he asked softly.

Tupper forced his best for-customers-only smile.

"Well, now, young sir, in the normal course of business, I usually don't sell them by the penny."

Toby's face fell.

"Oh . . . ." His voice was sharply edged with disappointment. Those peanuts smelled delicious, and it had been a long time since he had eaten any.

"However—" business had been brisk that morning and Tupper, in spite of himself, was feeling expansive, "seein' as how you're a handsome young rooster with cash money in hand, I devise I could part with, say, about six genuine plantation-grown Georgie goobers."

"Six?"

Tupper shrugged. "More'n you'd get if you bought 'em by the bag. That's a solemn fact."

Toby looked grave.

"Six, please," he said resignedly.

Harry Tupper wiped his hands and, with exaggerated care, selected six peanuts and handed them to Toby. He took the Indian head penny in exchange.

Toby squinted at one of the peanuts. He rolled it in his stubby fingers, regarding it gravely. A look of concern swept across his freckled face.

"You swap the ones back that are bad?" he asked.

Tupper's rather small eyes widened a bit.

"Bad?" He tried his best to look shocked and cried vehemently, "I don't vend bad peanuts in my establishment, boy. Maybe a little underbred, perhaps a little timeworn . . . ."

Toby shelled the peanut in question and took a bite. "*Tastes* bad," he said.

Impatience suddenly showed through Tupper's veneer of cheeriness. He leaned across the counter, hand outstretched.

"Here's two more," he said. "Now, run along. You'll miss the best part of the show."

Toby shrugged.

"Oh, I'm not going."

Keenly Tupper looked at him.

"Not going?" His voice was incredulous. Then understanding dawned on his crafty face. "Ah, you lack the price of a ticket?"

"Yes, sir."

His eyes still on Toby, Tupper scooped peanuts into a bag and twisted two more ears.

"I suppose your parents are bringing you tonight?"

Very carefully Tupper laid the sack on top of the stack

in the tray which was now in grave danger of toppling. How, he wondered, had his last boy managed to pile so many sacks on the tray without losing half of them?

He turned to reach for more bags. Toby bounded two steps, picked up the sacks, and handed them to Tupper.

"No, sir, I don't have any parents." Toby was eying the stack of popcorn sacks with concern. He began straightening it. To Tupper's surprise he saw that he could pile even more bags on it now without their falling off.

Tupper lifted a respectful eyebrow.

"Orphan boy, eh?" he asked softly.

Toby nodded, his fingers flying. He did not see the delighted look that flitted across Tupper's face, but he did notice that the man became even more friendly.

"Well!" Tupper was almost jolly. "Ever think of joining a circus, lad?"

Toby looked up, startled. He pointed a finger at himself and asked, "Me?"

Tupper expanded even further. In a melodramatic wave of his arm at the scene around them he went on persuasively, "Imagine being part of the glorious confraternity of the big top . . . ."

Looking down at Toby he was pleased at the wide-eyed delight on the boy's face and continued, "That exalted company of artistes who travel the length and breadth of this great land of ours . . . ."

Toby's eyes closed dreamily. They flew open when Tupper asked, "How would you like *that*?"

Toby gulped. "But what could I do?"

Tupper drew himself up grandly.

"You can become a concessionaire!"

"I could?" Toby was bewildered now. "A con-concess . . . ." He struggled manfully with the unfamiliar word but was forced to leave it dangling unfinished.

"Concessionaire!" Tupper lingered lovingly on every syllable. "Rolls out on the tongue mighty important, don't it?"

"Yes, sir," Toby agreed wholeheartedly.

Tupper quickly followed this up with, "Free transportation, a snug place to sleep, all you can eat, see the performance any time you please. Rub shoulders with the great and near great! And if that weren't enough, each Saturday night yours truly, Harry Tupper, will present you with one of these!"

Tupper fished into the right pocket of his striped

trousers and pulled out a big, round, shiny silver dollar. He held it up temptingly.

"What do you say, boy? Is it a bargain?"

Toby was silent for a moment. Then, slowly, he answered, "I guess I'd like that better than anything in the whole world."

"You would, eh?"

"Trouble is, Uncle Daniel and Aunt Olive need me—"

Tupper's expression changed with the speed of light.

"Aunt and uncle?" he asked sharply.

Toby nodded.

"They're awful poor," he said sadly, "and there's so much work I have to do for them around the farm."

Tupper's lips clamped to their usual thin line. Cool and offhand now, he said, "I understand, and it does you credit, my boy. I'm a loyal person myself, and I like to see it in others."

Toby looked up with eyes as sad as a hound pup's.

"I could ask 'em," he said.

Hastily Tupper scooped up more peanuts.

"Don't think another thing of it," he said, twisting the corners. "I'll pick up a boy in the next town. Plenty of them be glad to get such a golden opportunity."

"Yes, sir." Toby turned dispiritedly away. "Anyway, thank you."

Tupper, watching him through narrowed eyes, got another idea. "Just a minute," he said.

As Toby turned to face him, Tupper drew a wallet from his back pocket. He took a piece of paper from it, and with a stubby pencil drawn from the pocket of his striped shirt, he wrote something on it. He handed the paper to Toby.

The concessionaire was again his old, affable self where Toby was concerned.

"Just so's we part the best of friends," he said laughingly. "Here's a free pass to the performance tonight. Come and enjoy yourself, courtesy of Harry Tupper."

Unbelievingly Toby looked down at the paper. When he looked up his blue eyes shone like dew on the early morning grass.

"Mr. Tupper—I—" he stammered.

Mr. Tupper strapped the tray containing the sacks of peanuts and popcorn and the taffy apples around his neck. Without so much as another look at Toby he said, "Farewell, lad," and went toward the main tent. Soon, from the inside, Toby could hear his faint call: "Ice-cold

lemonade! It's pink! It's cold! It's refreshing!"

Toby took another long, loving look at the precious pass. With it he could see the show going on *inside* the tent. Uncle Daniel couldn't say NO to his coming back for the evening, not when it wouldn't cost a cent!

He turned and ran down the midway and out of the circus grounds. Soon he was on his way home.

He did not hurry. He stopped quite often to pick up a stone and throw it at nothing in particular. He jigged and spun around and whistled and sang and dreamed of the joys of the evening ahead.

Then, there was the shabby old house, across the barnyard from him. The latticed-in back porch was a pretty sight in the afternoon light, with the morning-glory vines strung up its side, hung thick with the blue-purple trumpetlike flowers.

Toby started across the yard. He saw Old Red with his nose buried in the water trough. Old Red saw him too. The weedy-looking old plow horse raised his head and nickered.

Toby threw his arms about Old Red's neck. He thrust the piece of paper Mr. Tupper had given him in front of the patient old horse's face.

"You know what that is, Red?" Toby asked breath-lessly. "A pass! A genuine free pass to the circus!"

Red's eyes sort of glazed over and it seemed he could see nothing special about the paper. He seemed to know he couldn't eat it, and if he couldn't eat it, what good was it?

Toby laughed and gave the old horse another hug. Then, whistling "In the Good Old Summertime," he hurried up the steps onto the latticed-in back porch and through its shady coolness to the back door of the kitchen.

Through the screen door he went. He turned to close it carefully as Aunt Olive always told him he should. As he did so he felt a hand on the collar of his shabby coat. He felt himself being jerked around with a swiftness that left him dizzy. He looked up—into the angry face of Uncle Daniel!

"Where have you been?" the old man demanded, his white brows meeting over the bridge of his long, thin nose.

Too scared to answer immediately, Toby let his eyes skitter over the familiar room.

Aunt Olive was bent over the old, blackened wood stove, stuffing a stick of wood into the round hole in the top,

from which she had just lifted the lid. Quickly she put
the lid back on and started stirring the contents of a kettle
on the back of the stove.

She worked with short, nervous motions, as she always
did at times like this. Toby could see, even from the side,
that her face was taut and strained. But she said nothing.

Uncle Daniel shook Toby, none too gently.

"I said: where have you been?" he growled.

Aunt Olive turned then and made a tentative step
forward, as though to stop her husband. Uncle Daniel saw
the move and glared at her. She stopped in her tracks.

Why didn't Aunt Olive talk up more to Uncle Daniel?
Instead, she seemed to drive her feelings in such matters
even deeper within her.

Roughly the old man let go of Toby's coat. "Answer
me!" he commanded.

Toby looked up, his eyes pleading for understanding.

"I'm sorry, Uncle Daniel," he gulped. "I meant to come
right back . . . but after the parade went by . . . I . . .
I . . . and then I happened to go to the circus grounds . . .
and a man gave me a free pass! Look!"

He held up the pass. Surely Uncle Daniel would see
what a wonderful thing it was. But the angry scowl on

the old man's face did not soften a bit.

Instead he roared, "Circus! Who did you expect to put the cow to pasture? Did you know the hogs broke down the fence because you didn't feed them, and rooted up the turnip field?" Uncle Daniel lowered his face until the tip of his nose almost touched Toby's short one. "Did you?"

Sudden tears welled up in Toby's eyes. As he shook his head, two big ones rolled down his cheeks.

Aunt Olive spoke up mildly. "Toby, we counted on selling that crop. You know how we need the money."

Her soft reproach brought overwhelming guilt to Toby. Hanging his head he wiped away another tear with the cuff of his sleeve. Numbly he heard Uncle Daniel say, "You're a shiftless, ungrateful boy!"

Miserably Toby looked up in time to see Aunt Olive take another step toward them, concern for the boy in her faded eyes.

"Now, Daniel," she reproved the old man gently, "don't be too hard on him. Boys get skittish when a circus is in town."

Uncle Daniel snorted and went on harshly, "He don't have a right to behave like other boys! He's got no rights at all, and he knows why!"

Aunt Olive gave a horrified gasp. Her timidity fled as she cried, "Don't say that to him!"

Uncle Daniel turned toward her. "Now, don't you stand up for him!" His anger rose with every word. "I got something to tell this boy and I mean to do it."

He turned back to Toby and continued in a voice cold with indignation, "My wife and I go without things we need to feed and clothe you. I'm a poor man, yet I took you in, out of decency's sake"—the words he added were like daggers to Toby's feelings—"when no one else would have you!"

"Daniel!" Aunt Olive's voice rose to an unprecedented high.

It didn't help any. Uncle Daniel kept right on.

"I don't know why we didn't send you to the county home in the first place. You're no kin to us. You're nothing to us, nothing but a millstone around our necks!"

Manfully Toby had been trying to hold back the tears. But now they burst forth and flowed freely down his freckled face. His shoulders shook with sobs.

"You don't mean that, Daniel," Aunt Olive cried, reaching forth a thin, work-worn hand as though to restrain her husband. But nothing, it seemed, could stem the tide of Uncle Daniel's anger. Fiercely he looked down at Toby and said, "Now, you just go up to bed and stay there. There'll be no place at supper for you."

Toby looked mutely from one old face to the other. His lips worked, but he could bring forth no words for his defense. He looked down at the circus pass the nice Mr. Tupper had given him.

Uncle Daniel's eyes followed the look and saw the pass. Grimly he yanked it from Toby's hand and tore it into tiny pieces.

With that Toby turned and walked, as fast as he could without seeming to run, toward the door to the hallway. There he mounted the stairs that led to his tiny room under the eaves.

Aunt Olive's words followed him.

"Those were cruel things to say."

Uncle Daniel's short reply echoed up the stair well. "Get on with the supper, Olive."

Toby did not see Uncle Daniel walk silently toward the door to the hallway nor the old man's eyes follow him as he climbed the last few steps. He was unaware of the uncertain look on his uncle's face, the look that asked, "Have I been too harsh with the boy?"

3 THE MILLSTONE

A few hours later the scene before Toby's bewildered eyes seemed one of wild confusion. Hugging to him a small bundle containing the few clothes he owned, the boy stood by the corner of a brightly painted wagon and looked uncertainly around.

It was night and the light of the torches, stuck at strategic spots around the circus grounds, illuminated the area enough so the roustabouts and their bosses could see what they were doing.

The evening performance was over. Colonel Sam Castle's Great American Circus was pulling up stakes and moving on to another village that had been plastered with posters announcing its coming.

Grotesque shadows, cast by moving men, animals, and wagons, danced about on the ground around Toby. Tents

44

were disappearing like magic, pulled down by shouting canvasmen. All around rose the cries of the animals, half-frightened despite the fact that they should have been well used to this routine by now. Horses neighed and whickered, elephants bellowed in protest at being made to haul and drag and do the heaviest work. From somewhere in the darkness came the weird, blood-curdling scream of a big cat.

"Heave there, boys, heave!" a man's voice bellowed from nearby almost as loudly as the elephants. Toby's eyes sought him out.

The bellow had come from the huge man he had seen in the parade, the one who had scowled back from the seat of the wagon that carried the monkeys and the mischievous chimpanzee.

Toby shuddered. He would stay away from that man, just as far as he could!

Still dressed in the striped cotton-knit shirt that emphasized his Herculean build, the man stalked toward the spot where Toby stood. Toby wanted to run. But somehow his feet felt glued to the spot.

Then Toby saw the two men who seemed to be having trouble pulling up a nest of ground stakes around which a guy line was fouled. Brusquely the big man strode up to the trouble spot and, seemingly without effort, pulled up the stakes. Then on he went toward another area, shouting as he did so, "Dutch! Clear that main falls rope!"

Toby stared at him. He appeared to be everywhere, helping, ordering, his eyes darting about checking up on details of the pulling-out job.

"Oley!" The big man's voice boomed again and Toby winced, it was so close. "Keep those cats covered when you move them!"

Toby started to move away from his vantage point by the wagon. Unconsciously he hoped to leave that big man, his scowl, and his booming voice behind him. Instead—

"Look out!" One could have heard that shout clear to Uncle Daniel's farm.

Startled, Toby looked around to see who the big man was hollering at now. Then he felt himself being suddenly lifted by the coat collar and held there, his feet dangling.

Toby sputtered angrily. He twisted around and looked at the spot where he had been standing just a few short seconds before. His gaze reached it in time to see the

sharp hoofs of a team of plunging horses dig into the hard-packed earth and send clods of it flying.

Frightened now, he looked up to see who had snatched him from in front of the runaway horses. It was the same big man and now he knew he had been hollering at a certain redheaded boy named Toby Tyler!

Then, as lightly as though he were discarding a peanut shell, the big man tossed Toby aside and strode on.

Indignation and gratitude struggled within Toby. Anger at being so callously treated was soon overcome by the sight of the still-plunging horses. If he had stayed where he had been before the big man picked him up so abruptly, he would be mincemeat now!

He had better get out of the way. He had not realized before that, while the circus was a wonderful place in many ways, it could be dangerous, too, with so many animals about.

A wagon stood nearby. Toby crept under it and cautiously came out on the other side. He looked up. The back of a familiar figure loomed before him. Toby sighed with relief. Mr. Tupper, the peanut, popcorn, and candy man! Just the person Toby was looking for. What a welcome sight!

Mr. Tupper was busily gathering up sacks and boxes and did not see Toby.

"Mr. Tupper!" Toby shouted as loudly as he could. The din all about them was too great. Mr. Tupper did not even turn around, but went right on picking up and packing away. Toby lifted both his hands and cupped them about his mouth.

"MR. TUPPER!" he yelled.

Mr. Tupper heard *that*. The concessionaire started nervously and some boxes tumbled to the ground. He turned and scowled angrily at the hopefully smiling boy.

"Here I am, Mr. Tupper," Toby said confidently.

"Well, what of it?" Tupper growled in answer.

For a second Toby was taken aback. This didn't sound like the pleasant, affable man he had talked to earlier in the day. Still . . . .

"Don't you know me? You said I could work for you."

Tupper's beady eyes narrowed.

"Oh?"

"I'm ready."

With great deliberation Harry Tupper put down one of the boxes he still held. He peered suspiciously at Toby.

"What about your aunt and uncle?" he asked.

Toby lowered his head. He did not want Mr. Tupper to see his trembling lip nor the way he had to fight to keep back the tears.

"They don't want me," he said grimly so as not to let the tremor in his voice be heard. Then he lifted his head in a gesture of defiance. "They said I was a millstone on their necks."

A look of satisfaction flicked across the crafty face of Harry Tupper. His attitude changed instantly to one of cordiality.

"All right. You got the job," he said, adding shrewdly, "fifty cents a week."

Toby's brows shot up. There was native shrewdness under his red thatch too.

"You said a dollar today," he said firmly.

It was Tupper's turn to look surprised. He thought for a moment. Then, realizing such astuteness on the part of a helper could have its advantages at times, he smiled faintly.

"If Harry Tupper said a dollar," he said grandly, "then a dollar it is. But don't you try running away after I spend my time teaching you the business."

Grinning broadly now, Toby rocked back and forth on

his heels. "No, sir," he promised.

Mr. Tupper grinned, too. This, he thought smugly, would be his lucky day. He held out his hand in a friendly gesture. Unhesitatingly Toby took it.

"Gentlemen's agreement." Harry Tupper's face was serious, as he added, "That's the most solemn thing there is. Understand?"

Toby's red head bobbed up and down.

Man and boy looked at each other in full agreement. Then Tupper said, "Now stay here and keep out of trouble. I'll be right back."

The concessionaire bent over and picked up a packing case. He started toward a wagon not far away.

"Mr. Tupper!" Toby's plaintive voice followed him.

Tupper turned his head but kept on.

"What?"

"I didn't have any supper tonight." Toby rubbed his stomach and sighed noisily.

Tupper's pleased expression changed to one of annoyance. For a second he had an urge to take a swing at the boy. The nerve of the kid!

Still, he had better play the part of Lord Bountiful for a few more hours, he guessed, until they were out of

Guilford. With reluctance he laid down the case he carried and went over to a tin box and scrabbled around in it. He came up with a banana almost black in color.

"Here you are, my boy." He handed it to Toby with all the flourish of a waiter setting a big, thick slice of juicy apple pie in front of him. "Nutritional gold from the Indies. See that it holds you till morning."

Toby took the banana with much less enthusiasm than that with which it was given. He knew a good banana when he saw one, golden in color with maybe a few brown flecks on its skin. But he was hungry enough to eat almost anything edible.

Clutching the fruit he backed away carefully, trying hard to keep out of the way of the busy, shouting men swarming all about him.

He stopped, thinking he was safe, in front of a wagon. He held up the banana and peeled down the blackened skin. He eyed the dark, bruised-looking flesh of the fruit. Sighing, he opened his mouth and aimed it at the fruit.

A small hairy fist whipped past his ear. It took hold of the banana and snatched it from the astonished Toby's grasp.

Toby whirled to stare at the bars of a cage on the

wagon behind him. Between them was the grinning face of a young chimpanzee holding his banana!

Indignation and anger swept across Toby's freckled face. The little thief! Toby's own hand whipped through the bars and grabbed the hairy fist.

The round little eyes of the chimp grew rounder. Clearly he hadn't expected this. Most kids had more sense than to thrust their hands through the bars of an animal cage. But what he didn't know was that most kids weren't as hungry as this one!

Toby tried to drag the chimp toward the bars. The chimp braced his big feet and resisted. Toby pulled harder. The chimp braced himself more determinedly. Then Toby started to win his strange tug-of-war. The chimp's feet, and the chimp, started sliding toward him.

Toby looked triumphant. The chimp looked concerned.

The chimp knew he had better do something about that banana, and quickly, or this angry human being might get it back. So he thrust it, skin and all, into his large mouth. His cheeks bulged.

Fury shook Toby to his foundations.

"You thief!" his voice rose shrilly. "Give that back!"

The chimp chewed twice, in answer, and swallowed.

The bulge disappeared. His mouth widened into an impish grin.

Toby gave the hairy hand an angry jerk. This brought the chimp indignantly toward the bars. Before Toby knew what was happening, the little animal was slapping his face and pulling his hair.

That wasn't all. The chimp opened his big mouth and proved he had a loud voice as well. His shrill chattering rallied all the others in the cage to his defense. There started such a violent outcry from all the other monkeys and chimps that it drowned out the noises about them.

Toby stared, open-mouthed. He let go the chimp's hand. Then he saw the big, burly man who had lifted him out of the path of the rampaging horses. Scowling deeply he was coming toward the monkey wagon!

Toby was frightened. How he wanted to run. But again his feet felt glued to the ground.

From behind him there arose a piteous wail. Toby turned and saw, on the floor of the cage, the chimp with whom he had fought for the banana. The chimp was holding up the fist he had grabbed, in a way that looked as though it had been crushed, and was emitting sounds that would have brought sympathy from a stone.

"Here! What's going on?" the big man bellowed. Then, seeing Toby by the cage, he grabbed him roughly. "Oh, it's you again!"

He shook Toby until his teeth chattered. Then he demanded, "What'd you do to that chimp?"

Toby's ire rose in spite of the man's size and fierce appearance. Outraged, he cried, *"Me?* I didn't do anything to him. First he stole my banana, then he started to pull my hair—" Suddenly it dawned on Toby: all the pain that chimp was feeling was phony! He glared at the writhing, howling animal. "Look at him! He's just pretending," he said disgustedly.

The big man looked. The chimp sent up a new series of cries, more piteous than those that had gone before. The big man's look sharpened as though he remembered having seen a display like this before. "All right, troublemaker. Settle down!" he said sternly to the chimp.

Then he let go of Toby.

"Now suppose you run home," he growled. "I'm getting tired of stumbling over you every time I turn around!"

Toby wanted to say something back, but somehow his tongue stuck to the roof of his mouth. That chimp! What a fraud he was!

From behind came a familiar and, to Toby, welcome voice. "What's the matter?" There was Harry Tupper, hands in pockets.

The big man grumped. "Boy here was getting the colonel's pet chimp riled up."

Tupper turned to Toby. "Thought I told you to stay out of trouble."

"He stole my banana!" Toby turned and pointed accusingly at the chimp who had given up his injured-paw act and was sitting there watching with satisfaction the going-over Toby was getting. Apparently feeling the withering scorn of Toby's look, the little simian yawned boredly. Then, insolently, he turned his back on the three humans who were getting so upset over him.

A clop, clop of hoofs nearby turned their heads. In awe Toby stared at the man astride the horse that stopped a few feet away from them.

Colonel Castle! What a fine figure he cut, sitting as stiffly as a ramrod astride his beautiful horse. Faultlessly attired, he seemed aloof from the hubbub about him. But he wasn't. That was plain when he turned toward Toby and Tupper and the big man and asked sharply, "What's wrong here?"

"Nothing, Colonel, nothing at all," Tupper answered hastily. "The monks just got a little excited."

Colonel Castle turned questioning eyes on Toby.

"Who's this?" he asked.

Toby thrilled right down to his toes. Imagine Colonel Castle taking notice, any notice at all, of him!

Tupper turned ingratiating. "He's my new helper, Colonel." Even Toby could see that his employer fawned shamelessly on the owner of the circus.

Castle, however, seemed unimpressed. Frowning, his eyes traveled over Toby, from his red hair to the toes of his stout brogans.

"Picking them kind of small, aren't you, Tupper?" he asked pointedly.

Nervously Tupper rubbed his hands together. "It's all right, sir. He doesn't have any folks, poor lad."

The concessionaire took several steps toward the man on horseback. Lowering his voice, he added confidentially, "I planned to take him under my wing"—he showed yellowed teeth in a tight-lipped smile—"give him a helping hand . . . ."

A look of distaste crossing his handsome features, Colonel Castle looked down at Tupper.

"Spare me your kind intentions, Tupper," he said hastily. He turned to the big man. "Let's get these wagons moving. The boy can ride up top with you, Ben."

That was the first time Toby had heard the big man called by name. He looked at him curiously.

Ben had turned to put up the sides of the monkey wagon. But at Colonel Castle's last words he whirled and let out a bellow.

"Thunderation, Colonel!" he howled. "Why pick me to wet-nurse Tupper's sniveling brats?"

Toby's dislike of Ben whatever-his-last-name-was soared. A sniveling brat, was he? He'd show that big elephant!

A millstone he had been to Uncle Daniel! A sniveling brat he was to Ben! He'd show them both!

Colonel Castle flicked his silver-studded reins and moved off unconcernedly.

"Trim your wagon, Ben," he said quietly as he left. "We're moving."

No sooner had Colonel Castle disappeared into the night than Ben glared down at the defenseless Toby. Toby stirred uneasily in spite of his determination to show Uncle Daniel and Ben that he was neither a millstone nor a sniveling brat.

Ben, however, said nothing to him. But the way he slammed the last board up on the side of the wagon told Toby what he thought of Colonel Castle's orders.

Toby gulped and turned to Mr. Tupper.

"Mr. Tupper," he said, "I think I changed my mind . . . ."

Tupper, for the first time, looked concerned over his new boy. He hastened to reassure him.

"Now, now, my lad, don't let our rough ways bother you none. We don't mean a thing by it, not a blessed thing."

To emphasize his point he fished into the pocket of his baggy coat and drew forth a grubby-looking paper bag. This he handed to Toby.

"Here," he wheedled, "I brought you some peppermint jaws to hold you till breakfast."

Toby looked down at the sack which held, at most, a half-dozen of the red-and-white striped candies. Should he, or shouldn't he? Was he, like Aunt Olive often said, jumping from the frying pan into the fire? Ben, that big man, had changed everything.

From far away it seemed to Toby came Colonel Castle's crisp command, "Move 'em!"

The crunch of moving wagon wheels came to Toby as he looked down at the paper bag trying to decide what he should do.

Then, suddenly, Tupper grabbed him and lifted him upward. Wildly Toby saw that he was on his way toward the seat of the monkey wagon. The broad, swarthy face of Ben leaned over the wheel and his big hands took Toby under the armpits and fished him upon the seat beside him. There he let the boy go so quickly that he sent Toby sprawling backward.

From the ground Tupper called, "You'll be snug as a mouse up there, lad. Mr. Cotter will be glad to take care of you."

Ben Cotter! So that was the big man's name!

Knowing it didn't help Toby's feelings any as he felt Cotter's glare upon him. Tupper waved reassuringly at him and scuttled away into the darkness.

He looked up again at Ben and decided right then and there he wanted no part of this angry, scowling man. Abruptly he started to scramble down from the seat. He felt Ben's grip again on the collar of his jacket.

"Colonel Castle says you ride with me," Ben said grimly, "you *ride*. Get a tight tailhold on yourself!"

Ben snapped the reins. The horses strained and the wagon started forward with a jolt. Toby's hand shot up to grab a leather strap hanging down from a little roof that curved over the seat to protect the driver from the elements.

The circus was moving and he, Toby Tyler, was moving with it!

4 A FRIEND IN CAMP

The monkey wagon, with Ben Cotter driving the team, moved into line with the other wagons and carts of the circus.

Clinging to the overhead strap, with Ben's grasp still tight on his arm, Toby experienced a sinking feeling in the region of his stomach. Here he was, with Colonel Castle's circus, moving out of Guilford and away from Uncle Daniel and Aunt Olive and all the things he had grown to know and love since he had come to live with them. Toby wasn't sure now whether he wanted to go or not. In fact, right this minute he was sure he didn't want to go.

Ben Cotter sat back beside him on the seat, his scowling face as dark as the night into which they were moving. Toby shuddered. Uncle Daniel's anger was fearsome but

Ben Cotter's was worse. Besides, he knew Uncle Daniel's bark was much worse than his bite. He knew nothing at all of this big, towering man beside him on the wagon seat.

He changed hands on the strap, the one in the air beginning to ache, at the same time sitting rigid and staring straight ahead into the darkness. They must be at the end of the string of vehicles, he decided, for there were so many of the tiny lanterns fastened to the ends of the wagons and carts ahead of them. Toby tried to count the bobbing lights, just to keep his mind off his troubles. But, appearing and disappearing as they did, it was like trying to count darting fireflies in the dark.

Out of the corner of his eye Toby could see Ben Cotter reach into the pocket of an old jacket lying on the seat and pull out the stub of a pipe. He watched the big man open a can of tobacco, shake some into the bowl of the pipe, and tamp it down with a huge forefinger. A match flared in the darkness, lighting up for a fleeting second Ben's dark face. The angry, disgruntled scowl was still there. The big man certainly resented his being here beside him, Toby reflected.

Puffing on his pipe and staring straight ahead, Ben

Cotter said gruffly, "Me, I don't like kids. Especially runaways. They're a weak-livered lot."

Toby choked back an angry answer. On second thought, perhaps it had been weakness that had made him leave Uncle Daniel and Aunt Olive and come with the circus. He hadn't wanted to leave Aunt Olive, who had always been kind to him. He would write to her and let her know where he was, he promised himself.

No, Toby thought, his jaw tightening. It hadn't been weakness on his part that had made him leave home. It was just that, well, he didn't want to be a millstone on anybody's neck. But Ben didn't know anything at all about what Uncle Daniel had said.

Ben went on, "Kid has a good home. First time some little thing goes wrong, he runs away. Then he finds things don't suit him just right—he wants to run home again."

Ben just didn't understand. A boy not only doesn't want to be called a millstone, he doesn't want to be called a sniveling brat either.

Toby leaned over and measured the distance from the wagon seat to the ground. He had jumped from a moving hay wagon once and it hadn't hurt him. Roll with the fall, that was the way to do it. Still, if there were big stones beside the road . . . he couldn't tell in the darkness.

Ben seemed to read his mind.

"Go ahead—jump!" the big man said grimly. "Nobody'll miss you. I doubt you're worth missing."

Toby aimed his fiercest glare at Ben, but said nothing.

"Jump!" Ben went on, taunting. "Don't be scared."

Toby's anger boiled over.

"I'm not scared!" he cried, his voice shrill with the fury he felt within him. He glared again at Ben and drew his brows together in what he hoped was a fearful scowl. "I'm not scared of you either."

Ben Cotter's features were as rigid as though carved in stone. Without even a flicker of change in expression he went on, "Fair enough, sonny."

Toby chose his next words carefully.

"Don't call me 'sonny.' My name's Toby Tyler."

"All right, sonny," sneered Ben. "We'll call you Toby."

If looks could hurt, Ben Cotter would have been a badly wounded man that minute. He went on, however, unconcernedly, "It's none of my business, but maybe you better catch some sleep. Morning comes mighty early with this outfit."

Toby's jaw set stubbornly. "Not sleepy," he retorted.

Ben shrugged. "Suit yourself."

Ben took a deep draw on his pipe and let the smoke drift from his mouth in lazy spirals.

Defiantly Toby folded his arms. His mouth changed to a lower-lip-out expression of indifference. He would just pretend the big man wasn't there. Stonily he stared ahead, forcing his eyes wider open than usual because he found that to be a good way of fighting off the drowsiness that was creeping up on him.

On the wagons went, the lights of the lanterns bobbing, bobbing . . . . In spite of his efforts Toby's head began bobbing, too, and very soon Ben Cotter noticed that his small companion was fast asleep, the curve of his light lashes falling on his rosy, freckled cheeks.

Funny, thought Ben, how like angels kids look when they're asleep no matter how aggravating they may be when awake.

The wagon lurched and swayed and, with each movement, Toby's small figure lurched and swayed with it. The wheels hit a deeper rut than usual and the front of the wagon dipped. Toby swayed forward, threatening to fall from his seat.

Ben's big hand quickly reached out and caught Toby under his chest and held him upright until the wagon had righted itself.

Then a look of resignation passed over Ben's rugged features. Oh, well, he was stuck with the kid, wasn't he? It wasn't the first time he had been stuck with one of Tupper's helpers. It wasn't easy for a kid alone in the world, without a real mother and father. He should know, he had been one himself. It seemed untold ages ago.

An old softy, that was what he was. Yet, not for anything would he show that side of him to the world. Long ago he had found the penalty for that was the scorn of his fellow workers, most of whom prided themselves on being tough.

And the kids . . . sometimes they had taken advantage of it. Though this redhead did seem different from the others, not whining or complaining like some, nor bragging and boastful like others.

From the seat beside him, Ben picked up his heavy woolen jacket and wedged it behind Toby's back. Then he pushed the boy, with a gentleness that would have amazed Toby if he had known, back against the garment, making his position on the wagon seat a little less precarious.

That done, Ben jammed his pipe back more firmly into his mouth. He turned up his collar against the chilliness of the night air and made himself as comfortable as possible for the long ride ahead.

Next morning Toby awoke with a start. He opened his eyes and looked sleepily around, rubbing the end of his nose. Something had hit him there.

He expected to see his room under the eaves of Uncle Daniel's house, the faded wallpaper, the washstand with its cracked pitcher and basin that didn't match, the mended curtains swaying in the breeze. Instead—

He shook his head briskly. Where was he, anyway? Under a tree out in the middle of nowhere? Now how had he got here? He had heard of magic carpets, but he was sure there were none around Guilford.

He was struck on the nose again, this time harder and sharper. It was a twig, a dried twig. Must have fallen from the tree above.

Another twig bounced off his head. He pulled himself to an upright position, still looking around dazedly. Now he knew those twigs hadn't fallen off any tree. They had been thrown at him. If this was somebody's idea of a joke . . . !

What was this wrapped around him? Ben Cotter's coat! How in the world . . . . Could it be? Things were more bewildering than before.

Another twig hit him. Toby jumped to his feet. His eyes came to rest on the monkey wagon, parked close to another tree. There, grinning at him from between the bars and pulling another twig from a nearby branch, was the chimpanzee who had snitched his banana! He could not mistake the markings on that chimp's face nor that impish, big-toothed grin.

Toby glared at the chimp. Then he cast his eyes around the ground for a small stone. He'd show that chimp how it felt to be hit on the nose with something!

He found a rock and hefted it with satisfaction. He raised his arm and was taking careful aim when, from around the corner of the wagon, Ben Cotter appeared. The swing stopped in mid-air. Toby whirled and, as though he had intended throwing it there all along, the rock sailed off harmlessly into the woods.

The chimp chuckled. Toby was sure he did. Anyway,

his broad grin appeared broader when Toby turned around again.

Around Ben's burly neck was a barley bag towel. Toby wondered silently where Ben was going. He remembered the jacket and felt better toward Ben. Still he found it hard to speak to the big man. He waited . . . .

Ben's voice was just as gruff as it had been the night before. "You'd better be up and doin', boy, before Harry Tupper comes looking for you."

Toby reached down and picked up the jacket. He brushed the dirt and twigs off it and handed it to Ben. He said, slightly embarrassed, "Thanks for taking care of me last night. Guess I fell asleep."

Ben's manner was brusque.

"Don't mean nothing to me one way or another. I didn't want you falling off the wagon and me getting blamed for it."

The warmth kindled in Toby's breast by the jacket vanished like a puff of smoke. Ben couldn't have hurt him more if he had slapped him in the face.

"I won't bother you any more," Toby said through stiff lips.

"I'm sure glad to hear that," Ben said heartily and

stalked off across the camping grounds.

Anxiously Toby looked around. He was in an alien, and, it seemed now, an unfriendly land. Where could he go? What could he do? Right now he wished he were back in Aunt Olive's kitchen eating the hearty breakfast she had always set before him. What if Uncle Daniel did glare at every bite he took? Toby had to admit there had been a lot of glares before he finished a meal.

There, at least, he had one friend, Aunt Olive. Here, he had none—no, that wasn't true. Where was Mr. Tupper?

Past the monkey cage he walked then, in his search. The chimp put his face between two bars and made a face at him, and, at the same time, made a noise that sounded like a raspberry. He would just show that chimp. He started to make a face back and then . . . well, the chimp didn't know any better. Aunt Olive had told him to mind his manners. Lifting his chin, he walked with dignified silence past the cage.

Whack! Another twig, a bigger one, hit him in the back of his head. Almost, but not quite, he forgot about dignity and minding manners. It wasn't easy but he managed to walk on, despite the raucous sound of simian laughter and gibberish following him.

Toby forgot the chimp, however, as he walked through the camp, now busy with early morning tasks. The wagons and carts had halted in a flower-strewn meadow beside a sparkling little stream. Beyond was a stretch of green woods from which came the musical sounds of many birds. The sun shone warmly down. Here and there a chipmunk scurried and eyed him beadily from behind a stone, or a squirrel flicked up a tree and scolded from a limb.

Men were hurrying back and forth and some of the women were down by the creek washing clothes, pounding them on stones and rinsing them and hanging them on bushes to dry.

Downstream the elephants and camels were being bathed and groomed and, elsewhere, horses were being curried and tethered out to graze in the lush green grass.

Toby started to whistle a cheerful tune. Now this was more like he had imagined circus life to be.

Ben was a little way ahead, striding on, looking neither to the right nor the left. Toby saw the rough towel slip from around the big man's neck and slide to the ground. Toby ran and picked it up and then raced around in front of Ben and handed it to him.

Ben didn't even thank him. Instead he just glared down at him as though he were some pesky, yapping stray dog nipping at his heels.

Disappointed, Toby turned away. Then he saw some members of the company smiling at the sight of big, tough Ben Cotter being followed by such a small boy.

For Ben had just grabbed the towel and strode on, while Toby had again fallen in behind him and trotted in his footsteps.

Two roustabouts guffawed and Toby saw Ben's shoulders stiffen. Then one of the men howled gleefully, "For a big fella he sure throws a puny shadow! Don't he, Lafe?"

"Sure does."

The first roustabout followed his witticism with, "Say, Lafe, think I ought to tell him his apron strings is draggin'?"

Ben seemed to growl under his breath like a dog being tormented by small boys.

The laughter continued. It followed Ben and Toby for perhaps two or three steps farther. Then Ben stopped abruptly, so much so that Toby almost stepped on his heels. Slowly the big man turned, and brushing past Toby, started for the first roustabout. The astonished man, no puny fellow himself, soon found himself hanging by the slack of his shirt in mid-air. Holding the squirming roustabout well out ahead of him, Ben headed toward a water trough from which an elephant was still drinking. Into the water Ben threw the man, as easily as if he had been a straw.

Ben turned to the second roustabout.

"I didn't say anything," the threatened one said hastily and backed away from the big man.

Ben, apparently satisfied that he would be laughed at no longer, resumed his walk toward the stream.

His eyes wide with surprise, Toby fell in and trotted behind him. My, what a temper Ben had! What muscles, too!

Reaching the bank of the stream Ben turned and glared. Toby, however, had stopped a safe distance away.

"I—I—I was wondering where to wash up," he said, as though trying to explain his presence there.

Ben made a sweeping gesture toward the stream.

"That's water, ain't it?"

"Yes, sir."

"All right. Now do me a favor and keep out of my way."

Ben turned and walked on down the stream almost to the place where the elephants and camels were being soaped and scrubbed.

Toby followed him there, almost. A few feet away from Ben, Toby bent over the water and splashed some gingerly on his face. Then he stopped and looked at Ben who was taking his washing much more seriously.

Ben, seeing his look, asked irritably, "What's the matter?"

"You sure got a bad temper, mister."

Ben snorted, sending soap and water flying.

"Don't let that bother you," he growled, and leaning over he splashed water all over his face and neck and into his thick, black hair. He straightened then and started rubbing the washed areas with the rough towel. "You're working for Harry Tupper, a real fine fellow."

Toby bridled at the tone of the big man's voice as he bit off the last four words.

"Anyway, he's friendly."

Ben grinned broadly, showing large, white, even teeth. Too bad he didn't grin more often, Toby thought. Then

Toby realized that Ben saw something he didn't.

"Sure thing," Ben said, "and by a happenstance, here's Mr. Friendly himself come looking for you."

Toby whirled and, sure enough, there was Mr. Tupper coming down the bank toward him. Toby's heart sank. On the face of the concessionaire was a sour, unpleasant scowl.

"What's the idea making me chase all over camp for you?" Tupper snarled at Toby.

Toby tried to smile but the results were poor.

"Morning, Mr. Tupper. I was just washing up."

Tupper grabbed Toby, yanked him away from the edge of the water.

"Not on my time, you aren't! Come on! Move along!"

Toby hoped Ben hadn't seen this. The big man seemed absorbed now in scrubbing his hands and arms and elbows. But, from what Toby could see of it, there seemed to be a grin on Ben's face.

Tupper gave him another rough shake.

"We don't want to be woolgathering all over camp when there's work to be done, do we?"

Toby stumbled and fell. Tupper yanked him to his feet. Out of the corner of his eye, Ben was watching.

Don't take it too far there, Tupper, old boy, he seemed to be thinking.

Gripping Toby by the arm and yanking him along, Tupper started back up the bank. He seemed to neither know nor care that Toby couldn't match his stride.

Ben sighed audibly and started after the concessionaire and the boy.

Toby felt the grip on his own arm lessen. He turned to see Tupper yanked into the air by Ben, and held there.

"Let me down!" Tupper cried indignantly.

"Sure, Mr. Tupper, sure," said Ben. "Just don't unsettle yourself."

Toby looked frightened.

"Let him down please," he pleaded, tugging on Ben's sleeve. "It was my fault."

Ben looked down at him, not unkindly.

"Stay out of this, boy. It's got nothing to do with you."

Tupper's face was purple.

"Take your dirty hands off me!" he screamed.

"I aim to," Ben answered laconically as he turned and walked back toward the stream, Tupper still held at arm's length.

"Now, Mr. Tupper, I don't believe in coddling," Ben

lectured as he went, "but I got my fill of you mistreating those helpers before breakfast every morning. It don't sit well with me."

"The boy works for me!" Tupper said, kicking furiously. "I'll do as I like with him!"

They were by the stream now. Ben held Tupper out over it.

"Sure, Mr. Tupper," he said softly, "you just tell him what you want him to do. If he don't do it, you can fire him. But if I ever catch you roughing him up again, I'm liable to do something like this . . . ."

Ben let go. Tupper hit the stream with the grace of a water buffalo.

Ben turned toward Toby. "As for you," he said sternly, "you listen to Mr. Tupper. Work hard and do your job right. He's your employer and you be respectful to him. Understand?"

"Yes, sir," Toby gulped.

Ben went on, "Now you can go to work soon's you had your breakfast. The cook tent is over there."

Ben waved at a tent over close to the line of trees, from which mouth-watering smells of food were beginning to come. Toby turned and started toward that tent.

Ben's voice followed him as he went, "Why, you're all wet, Mr. Tupper. Here!"

Toby turned his head just enough to see Ben throw his towel to the concessionaire who was emerging from his unwanted bath, shaking and sputtering. Toby saw the evil look Tupper sent after Ben as the big man walked off, whistling.

Confused, Toby went on toward the cook tent. Did he, or did he not, have a friend in this camp?

5 MILLSTONE MONEY

The delicious aroma of cooking food, coming to Toby from the cook tent, became even more tempting as he neared it. One deep sniff at the door almost made him forget his troubles of the morning.

He paused and looked about. At one of the plank tables, strewn about the large enclosure, sat three clowns. In costume, but without make-up, they didn't look a bit funny this morning.

At another table were several bandsmen in their bright blue uniforms generously decorated with gold braid and epaulets. Beside them, intent on the tin plates before them, were two performers in spangled tights with robes thrown over their shoulders.

There were others there, barkers, performers, and roustabouts.

Behind another long plank table, filled with steaming pots and pans and kettles, stood a cook in white apron and tall white hat. With ladles and forks he was filling the plates of those passing by from the heaps of food before him. A tiny lady in full short skirt and a golden crown on her head was just leaving the table carrying a full plate and steaming cup. Toby recognized her as the one he had seen riding on the elephant yesterday.

"Here, boy!" the cook called. Toby turned and looked around. Then he realized that the cook was calling him.

Happily he made his way to the chow table. As he drew up in front of it, the grinning cook picked up a large tin plate and, while Toby watched with hungry eyes, filled it with scrambled eggs, ham, hot cakes, and big chunks of bread. Then, with a flourish, he handed the heaped-high plate to Toby.

Toby almost staggered under its weight. He looked around for a place at one of the other tables.

"Why don't you sit over here?" a sweet, lilting voice came to him from across the tent. Toby turned toward the speaker and almost dropped his plate. It was the pretty little equestrienne who had waved at him while he had been clinging to that lamp post!

He must be dreaming. Surely he would awaken soon and find that his heaping plate of wonderful food and the dainty, smiling girl did not really exist.

"Better hurry! It's almost time for parade assembly!" the voice came again. It was real all right and so was the smell of the food on his plate.

Dazedly, but with great caution so as not to spill anything while that dazzling girl was looking, Toby made for the table.

Alongside the table where she sat was a bench. Gingerly Toby sat down on one end of it, as far from the girl as he could get. He felt shy and awkward. Just looking at her made him feel all thumbs, with every one tied in a bandage.

Her hair, Toby thought, was the color of corn silk and just as shiny. Straight bangs covered her wide brow and two buns were braided over her small ears. Atop her head a golden tiara sparkled.

Her eyes were big and blue as cornflowers. When she smiled she sent Toby into a real spin.

A flowered silk robe was draped across her shoulders, covering her riding costume. She was Toby's idea of a perfect circus queen!

Toby had been so intent on the girl that he had not seen the filled plate that sat on the table between them. Nor did he see the boy in equestrian costume approach their table until the lad set a glass of milk beside the girl's plate and one by the plate in the center.

Toby knew right away who the boy was. He was the one who had ridden beside the girl in the parade. A feeling of resentment arose in Toby. The boy was even more handsome seen close up, dark, with classical features, and with hair waving back from a high forehead. And he moved with the grace and aplomb of one long accustomed to all this opulence and sure of his place in it. He wore a cape, too, and it gave him a foreign, exotic appearance that put Toby on the defensive. Beside this handsome creature Toby felt like a real hayseed.

The boy sat down in front of the third plate. Turning toward the girl he asked loudly, "Who's that, Jeanette?" And he jerked a fork in Toby's direction.

Toby hadn't liked the boy when he had seen him in the parade. He liked him less now.

Jeanette turned her blue eyes on her companion and answered coolly, "I don't know, Ajax."

So those were their names, Jeanette and Ajax. And he

had to have a name like Toby!

Jeanette leaned forward a bit so she could see around Ajax and, looking squarely at Toby, she asked sweetly, "You're new, aren't you?"

Ajax looked at Toby, too, a coldly appraising look. "You're not supposed to sit here, you know," he said, haughtily. "This table is for performers."

Annoyance swept across Jeanette's face. Her blue eyes snapped.

"Stop it, Ajax," she said sharply. "I asked him to sit down."

Toby smiled nervously. Feeling more awkward than ever, he picked up his fork and slid it under a generous portion of scrambled eggs. But, in lifting it to his open mouth, his hand jerked for some unaccountable reason, and the food plopped back into his plate.

Ajax eyed him with disgust. He threw a look at Jeanette that seemed to say, "The big oaf!"

Grimly Toby tried again. This time, with more careful balancing, he succeeded in putting the food into his mouth. Those eggs and ham and hot cakes tasted wonderful! Toby savored them with unabashed enjoyment.

Such boorish enjoyment of food seemed to infuriate

Ajax. He grabbed hold of Toby's arm and pulled, hard.

"Did you hear what I said?" He jerked on the arm again. "And look at me when I'm talking to you!"

Ajax spoke so loudly that almost everyone in the tent looked their way. Among them, standing in the chow line, was a mild-looking, balding man in striped dressing jacket. His painted-on brows came together in a frown. His eyes and those of the cook's met in a look of resignation as the cook continued to pile the plate he held with scraps.

The voice of Jeanette came to them then.

"Oh, Ajax," she cried in annoyance, "let him alone!"

Both the men at the chow table nodded, pleased. Jeanette's true colors were showing this morning, as well as those of Ajax. Her kindness and consideration were as evident as the boy's unpleasantness. Though she was one of the star attractions of Colonel Castle's Great American Circus, she was never haughty or arrogant about it.

But that Ajax!

His plate piled even higher than the others, the mild-looking man smiled his thanks at the cook and turned away from the chow line.

Toby did not see the man near their table. All he could

do was hear Ajax cry angrily, "He's not supposed to be at our table! Go on, take your plate and go!"

Ajax gave him a push then that almost sent the embarrassed Toby off the bench. But Toby quickly righted himself, and picking up his plate, he rose to leave. He still had some pride!

Toby felt his plate being lifted out of his hands.

"There you are, my boy!" said the man with the kind face and painted-on brows, holding his full plate in one hand and Toby's in the other. "Colonel Castle particularly asked me to look out for you!"

Toby looked up, bewildered. First he couldn't eat with the performers and now Colonel Castle . . . . Did Colonel Castle still remember the boy who had joined the circus the day before?

"Huh?" he asked blankly.

The man winked at him and indicated a table not far away.

"I want you to be a guest at my table," he said, loud enough for everybody to hear. "Come over here and meet some of your new colleagues."

They walked past Jeanette and Ajax. Jeanette, Toby noted, looked pleased; but Ajax looked astonished—so much so that Toby wondered just who this kind man was.

The man put Toby's plate down on a table in a corner and set his own down beside it. Toby looked at the plate the man had carried and his eyes widened. Did he *like* scraps?

Nonplused, Toby sat down. Some of the others already there looked at him curiously.

The man, however, remained standing. He looked at the others at the table and said with great dignity, "Ladies and gentlemen, may I present—"

He leaned over and asked Toby, "Are you taking a professional nom de plume this season, or do you plan to use your own name?"

Then he paused delicately.

Toby looked at him, more bewildered than ever.

"Er—my own, I guess, sir," he stammered. "Toby Tyler."

"Toby Tyler, why not? A fine name. I've always liked it. Ladies and gentlemen, you've all heard of Toby Tyler!"

The others politely inclined their heads in acknowledgment. Toby, to cover his confusion, began to eat.

The man tapped Toby lightly on the shoulder. With a

wave of his hand he indicated a handsome woman sitting across the table.

"The beautiful lady," he said grandly, "is *Signorina* Zorelda, queen of trapeze and the upper regions of the air."

Halfway to his mouth Toby's fork stopped. The *Signorina* was beautiful indeed, in a dark, flashing way. But more awesome to Toby was the realization that she was one of the performers who worked in the rigging in the top of the tent, flying from one swinging trapeze to another, their split-second timing the only factor keeping them from plunging down, down, down.

Signorina Zorelda favored him with a pleasant smile and went back to her own eating.

Toby's new friend nodded toward a man sitting by the *Signorina,* a short, dynamic-looking fellow with thick black hair that curled in tight ringlets to his round head. This man was eating with his knife! It was plain he had never had an Aunt Olive to tell him to use his fork.

"The Great Orcata—" Toby's friend said.

The Great Orcata raised his curly-haired head and nodded. But he kept right on eating and, to Toby's horror, the blade of the knife disappeared right down the man's throat! Orcata didn't even seem to notice as his white teeth, beneath a formidable black beard, showed in a wide smile.

"—sword swallower extraordinaire," finished Toby's friend.

Toby howled. He was a hayseed all right and a pretty dumb one at that.

The Great Orcata gave him a broad wink and looked pleased with himself.

His laughter had attracted the attention of everybody in the tent. To cover his embarrassment, Toby took a bite of bread and chewed rapidly.

His friend waved at a heavy-set, blond fellow with large, outstanding ears who was covered, every inch of him that showed, with pictures of ships and birds and flags and palm trees. "Mr. Bogliostro, the tattooed man," he said, and passing to the man next to him, "Mr. Phillips, who is in charge of the menagerie, and," at the end of the table was a long, thin man with drooping white mustaches and a sad look, "Professor Corbett, *maestro* virtuoso of the steam calliope."

Then Toby's mild-mannered friend leaned over and said confidentially, "I am Sam Treat, circus clown."

"A clown?" Toby asked in an awe-choked voice. No wonder Ajax had been surprised that this fellow had befriended a ragged nobody like himself. Clowns and elephants were really the most important parts of a circus.

The clown, in a funny Dutch accent, went on, "At your zurvice!" Then he saluted and almost jabbed himself in the eye. "Ow!"

Toby laughed. Sam Treat was doing his best to make him feel at ease and he knew it.

"Und vot do *you* do mit the zircus, Mr. Tyler?"

Toby gulped. Then he remembered what Mr. Tupper had told him.

"I'm a—a constashunaire!" he said boldly.

Sam Treat looked a bit taken aback. Then he brightened.

"Constashunaire? Ah, yes. Vair vould the zircus be midoudt them!"

From somewhere outside a bugle sounded, sweet and clear. Toby saw *Signorina* Zorelda rise and hurry out.

Orcata rose, too, and sort of waddled out, he was so fat. The tattooed man followed with the rolling gait of one who had spent a great deal of his life on shipboard.

At Toby's puzzled look Sam Treat smiled and said, "That's the thirty-minute parade alert." Then he added,

"I've got to get breakfast to my family."

"Why?" Toby asked wonderingly. "Don't they eat here?"

His eye on the plate of scraps Sam Treat had brought with him, Toby finished his own food. Somehow he felt sure the clown had eaten earlier, right here in the cook tent. Now would he feed his family on scraps?

Toby wished he had brought a glass of milk to the table, as Ajax had done. He should have asked for one, probably. Well, he would learn. Next meal he would ask for a glass of his favorite beverage. He smacked his lips and sighed contentedly. This meal was a big improvement over Mr. Tupper's peppermints. He pushed himself away from the table.

"I'm afraid not," Sam Treat said in answer to his question. The clown picked up the plate of scraps and made ready to leave. "Would you care to meet them?"

"Sure," Toby said eagerly and he got up and started to follow his friend.

Jeanette smiled at him when he looked back at the table where she still sat with Ajax. The young equestrian leveled a scowl at him. "Young upstart," Toby thought, "that's what he thinks I am."

Out of the cook tent went Sam Treat and Toby, across a grassy spot to another small tent. Toby skipped happily alongside his new friend.

"How large a family do you have, Mr. Treat?" he asked.

Sam lifted the flap of the tent and held it up so Toby could go through the opening.

"Oh, most of the time it averages between four and five," he said.

Toby looked puzzled but, trying not to show it, he went into the tent. Sam followed him.

It was a dressing tent with a mirror hanging on a center pole. There was a table along one side with eight plates on it! Toby stared. What kind of a family could this be? He wondered even more as Sam Treat carried the heaped-up plate he had brought from the cook tent over to this table and divided the scraps among the eight plates.

"All right, kids," he cried, *"now!"*

The round tops of eight small trunks, scattered about the tent, suddenly flew open. Out of each trunk popped a small dog!

The animals dashed toward the tables and the plates.

They were of many descriptions, long-eared, short-eared, black and white and brown and spotted. In only one thing were they exactly alike. They were all hungry!

Toby howled again. When he could stop laughing, he said, "When you said you had a family, I thought . . . ."

Sam smiled at him and said quietly, "No, I don't have a regular family, Toby. This is about the best I could do."

Toby grinned cheerfully, patting one of the little dogs on the head.

"I don't have a regular family either. That's why I joined the circus. I ran away, you know."

Sam Treat now stood in front of the mirror on the pole. In his hand was a glass jar full of red grease-paint. Unscrewing the top he said, smilingly, "Really? I never would have guessed it."

He turned a sympathetic eye on the boy rocking back and forth on his heels trying to make Sam think he really didn't care one way or the other. The clown shrugged. "Oh, well, you'll be missed for a little while, maybe." He turned back to the mirror and smeared some of the red paint about his lips. "But they'll get over it."

Toby had had the feeling all along that he had seen Sam Treat before. Now he remembered. It had been

Sam who wordlessly scolded him yesterday when the parade was going by. It had been Sam's little dogs that had been dressed up like miniature elephants! Sam was painting on his face the same wide-lipped mouth that Toby remembered had worked so hard and said nothing. He couldn't forget that mouth!

"It wasn't because they didn't want me." He stopped rocking and said defensively, "But they're awful poor. I was just a millstone on their necks."

Gravely Sam Treat watched Toby from his mirror.

"Millstone, eh?" He twisted his mouth this way and that to be sure he had it painted on just right. "And you're never going back?"

Toby thought that over for a second while he patted another dog on the head. He straightened up and sighed.

"Guess not. Leastways, not till I earn some money to take back so I can show them I wasn't what my uncle said I was."

Sam put the jar down inside a make-up box full of jars and cans and small boxes. He fished around in it until he found an old leather pouch. He tossed it to Toby.

"You know, Papa Schultz used to say," he lapsed into his funny Dutch way of talking, "happiness you could schpend around, und it comes back more so. Money, you should keep it in something."

"Papa Schultz?"

"An old clown I used to know. I wanted to make people happy the way he did. That's why I went off with the circus."

"You ran away too?"

Sam Treat nodded.

"Papa gave me this pouch to save money in. He said, 'The zircus iss for elephants and Papa Schultz. Everyone else should take the money und go home!'"

"But *you* didn't." Toby poked the pouch into a pocket.

"Save your money, Toby," Sam went on. "Don't wait till it's too late."

"Thank you, Mr. Treat. I'll work real hard. I'll do everything Mr. Tupper tells me. Oh, my gosh!"

"What's the matter?"

"I forgot about Mr. Tupper waiting for me! 'By!"

"Come back and see us. We're always glad to have company," Sam called after him.

6   A HARD JOB

The afternoon performance had begun.

Signorina Zorelda stood poised, slim and lovely, on a platform high above the heads of the audience. With one hand she lightly swung a trapeze back and forth before her.

From another platform, on the other side of the center ring, two muscular men in tights had swung their trapezes off into the space at the top of the tent. Hanging on them by their knees, they were now swaying back and forth, heads down and arms extended.

The crowd waited expectantly. The music of the band, soft at first, rose to a crescendo. Suddenly, drums rolling, the *Signorina* grasped her trapeze as it swung back to her. An instant's wait until her catchers were in time with her and she swung off into space toward them.

Back and forth she went, twice, and then she let go her own trapeze. She did a graceful forward somersault in mid-air, and was caught by the wrists by the man swinging toward her!

The crowd gasped.

If the timing had not been perfect, she would have plunged into the safety net below. Those nets weren't as safe as the name implied. A performer had to know just how to land in one or he could wind up with a broken neck!

It was the first time Toby had seen the show. He stood in the aisle, eyes wide and mouth agape. *Signorina* Zoreida's act was as new and thrilling to him as it was to the audience.

Hung from a strap around Toby's neck was a big tray on which sat a pitcher filled with lemonade. Around the pitcher sat glasses and bags of peanuts and taffy candy.

There was nothing hard about the selling end of Toby's job. Nothing, that is, but trying to see what was going on in all three rings, waiting on customers, and keeping that pitcher and the glasses from sliding off the tray, all at the same time!

So far he had done quite well. He had managed to see

Signorina Zorelda fly through the air to be safely caught
by the man swinging toward her. A split second before
that he had watched the seal act in the ring on his left.
One seal had tossed a big rubber ball from the tip of his
nose to the tip of another seal's nose just as Toby's head
had swung around and caught the flying act in the center
ring.

Signorina Zorelda was swinging back and forth, grasp-
ing the first catcher's wrist, as Toby's head pivoted to the
ring on his right. There, in a cage, a man armed with
a whip and a chair was putting five tigers through their
paces. At the sound of the snapping whip one tiger after
another leaped from the top of a barrel through hoops and
back again!

Another drum roll and Toby's head whipped back to
the center ring. He was just in time to see *Signorina*
Zorelda leave the first catcher, swing through the air doing
a double forward somersault, and grasp the wrists of the
second catcher as he came toward her!

The pitcher on Toby's tray began to slide. He saw it
and righted it, just in time.

Wow! The circus was a thrilling place! Between gasps
of mingled horror and amazement the audience was send-

ing up thunderous rounds of applause. Toby wanted to applaud, too, but couldn't, not with that tray on his chest!

His eye was caught by something else, the figure of Harry Tupper approaching. With short angry steps Tupper was upon him before he could move away, gesturing to him to get busy. Hastily Toby started up an aisle between the plank seats.

"Ice-cold lemonade! Here you are, folks! Five cents a glass! It's cold and refreshing!"

Another roll of drums sounded. Toby's back stiffened. *Signorina* Zorelda was going through another hair-raising maneuver and Toby knew it. But he did not dare turn around. He could feel Harry Tupper's eyes still on him. So he poured a glassful of lemonade and passed it down the row of spectators to a customer. Then he waited for his nickel.

Business was brisk. It was a hot day and the air inside the tent was sweltering. His pitcher was empty in no time.

As he hurried down the aisle for a refill, he saw *Signorina* Zorelda and her two catchers on the ground, bowing to a wildly applauding crowd. Behind them roustabouts were striking the safety net and another act,

Toby saw on leaving the tent, waited in the back door to make its entrance.

When Toby returned, his pitcher full, he tried hard to keep his eyes turned away from all the exciting activity in the rings below the stands. He could not watch the show, he grimly told himself, and sell his wares at the same time. And he had vowed to work hard, do as Mr. Tupper told him, and save his money!

In spite of his good intentions he caught a glimpse of several liberty horses racing around the track. And between steps up the aisle he could tell that three clowns had come in and were doing walk-around "bits."

It was out of the corner of his eye that he saw another single clown come in. He knew it was Sam Treat. He didn't know why he knew it, for the costume and the make-up hid the man inside. But Toby *knew*.

He just *had* to watch his friend's act. Just for a second, he promised himself. And he turned about.

Sam was walking around in front of the audience. Suddenly he spied a blue handkerchief lying on the ground. He stopped and looked at it and then went on a couple of steps. Then he returned to it and timidly picked it up.

Without a word Sam made it clear to the crowd that he was trying to find the owner of the blue handkerchief. Then, as he and the crowd watched, amazed, the handkerchief changed color! Right before their eyes it changed from blue to bright red!

Apparently scared out of his wits Sam dropped the handkerchief. Quickly he turned as though to run away. As he did so he bumped into the clown magician.

The magician waved a hand and the handkerchief disappeared into his own hand. How wonderful! Sam applauded the feat of magic as wildly as did the crowd.

Whereupon the magician reached into Sam's pocket and pulled out the red handkerchief. He turned and bowed.

Sam, not to be outdone, tried to do the same trick. He reached into the pocket of the magician's coat and tugged and pulled. What looked like the end of the red handkerchief finally appeared.

Sam kept on pulling. The red "handkerchief" kept getting bigger—until it turned out to be a suit of long red underwear! Sam and the magician gave it a look of complete surprise. Then both did a funny little hop. The act ended with the magician chasing Sam out of the tent.

The crowd howled and so did Toby, louder than any of them.

A pleased smile on his face, Colonel Castle stepped out and shouted, "Ladies and gentlemen, your kind attention, please! The Great American Circus now proudly presents a three-way extravaganza! On the north platform—the mighty Benjo."

Toby had to find out who *he* was! His gaze followed in the direction of Colonel Castle's sweeping arm and came to rest on Ben Cotter! Toby couldn't mistake that big, burly build nor the dark scowling face with the odd side-whiskers! Ben was all dressed up in a sort of Roman gladiator outfit and was lifting some tremendous weights above his head. Toby just had to see his act.

Ben bowed. The crowd clapped. Colonel Castle went on, "On the south platform—the peerless Ojita, direct from the mysterious inscrutable land of the Orient."

Toby turned quickly toward the south platform. There he saw a man with slanting eyes, dressed in a costume that could have come straight from the land of the Arabian nights. His paraphernalia indicated that he was a juggler. He bowed with great solemnity, as though to an emperor. Toby couldn't miss that!

Watching, Toby drew in a deep ecstatic breath. To think that he, Toby Tyler, who only yesterday had been one with the audience of common, everyday folk, was now a member of this exotic, glamorous group of people drawn from all parts of the world!

Again Colonel Castle's voice sounded above the hubbub. "And in the ring, those towering titans of terpsichore, the wonder of the pachyderm world—Dinsmore's Dancing Elephants!"

Into the center ring lumbered several elephants. To the slow beat of a band number and the waving stick of their trainer, they lifted first one foot and then another and swayed from side to side in something that could have resembled dancing.

Toby's gaze went back to Ben. How thrilling it was to think that he had ridden on the same wagon seat with that huge man there on the platform performing before all these people.

Ben hadn't said a word to him about being the circus strong man. Toby would have thought he'd be bragging about it all the time. Ben was not only big and strong and brave, he was also modest.

Ben had a curved bar across the back of his neck. To

each end of the bar a Shetland pony was fastened by a belt under its middle.

Toby could see the muscles in Ben's short neck fairly bulge as the strong man strained to lift those ponies off the ground.

The audience groaned with him, it seemed, as he sweated and puffed with the effort. A roll of drums sounded and then, ever so slowly, the tiny hoofs of the ponies began to leave the ground. What muscle! What strength! If they weren't seeing it with their own eyes the folks in the audience would never have believed it, nor would Toby.

Inch by inch Ben's shoulders straightened and the bar and the ponies went up with them. Then, with Ben upright, and the ponies swinging on the ends of the bar like the buckets of a Dutch milkmaid, another marvelous thing happened. The ponies began turning round and round like wooden horses on a merry-go-round. On the ends of the bar were mechanisms that Ben controlled with pressure on a button. Round and round went the ponies, as gracefully as birds in flight.

The audience clapped and cheered. Toby would have clapped, but again he remembered the tray and the pitcher

of lemonade, just in the nick of time.

Pride swelled within Toby, fit to burst. He just *had* to tell someone. So he nudged the fellow in the striped suit and the round straw sailor hat who stood next to him.

"He's a friend of mine!" Toby whispered excitedly, nodding toward Ben. The strong man was now standing on the platform making the ponies go round and round.

The man he nudged shot a surprised, or was it envious, glance at Toby. Toby had never been so happy in his life.

His happiness disappeared like a puff of smoke. Glancing down the aisle he saw Tupper standing at the bottom, scowling and gesticulating.

Toby leaped into action. He tore his eyes away from the shows in the rings and hastily climbed farther up into the stands.

"Lemonade!" he cried, just as loud as he could holler.

Down below, Dinsmore's Dancing Elephants were lumbering through a polka, though actually no one could tell just what *kind* of a dance it was except the band was playing a polka.

Resolutely Toby shut his eyes and ears to the sights and sounds of the big show. Industriously he moved among the members of the audience, shouting his wares and pouring lemonade and making change and trying not to spill any of the cold liquid down anybody's neck. And that wasn't easy with all the joggling and moving about that was going on, with folks standing and craning their necks for better views.

Out of the corner of his eye, though, Toby managed to glimpse Ojita, lying flat on his back on the platform in the ring and spinning a barrel round and round with his feet. The mysterious Oriental even tossed the spinning barrel into the air and caught it again as it came down. Then he continued spinning it again just as though nothing had happened.

A voice from the middle of one of the plank seats sent Toby's attention back to his job.

"Four glasses of lemonade—" a lady was saying, "not too sweet—a candied apple, and three bags of peanuts."

Toby looked her way and nodded. He began filling the mother's order for herself and children and wished he were a centipede or something, so he would have more hands.

He poured the lemonade into the glasses, not adding any more sugar like some customers demanded, and carefully passed them one at a time down the line of people who sat on his side of the lady. Courteously, if absent-mindedly, the people between passed the glasses on down the line. Toby held his breath until they reached their destination. Not a drop was spilled though it had been close a couple of times. Then he sent down the candied apple and the bags of peanuts.

After that he stood, first on one foot and then on the other, while the lady fished into an enormous pocket-book and came up with a dollar bill. This she passed down to him.

Toby waited for the dollar to reach him. Then he sent back sixty cents in change and waited again. When he saw the lady had received it, counted it, and put it into her purse, he moved on.

Behind him the elephants had finished their dance and were leaving the ring. Ben and the juggler had gone through their routines and were bowing and making ready to leave too.

It was a hard job for Toby to keep his back turned away from all that the crowd seemed to be enjoying so much. But this time he did. He kept right on passing out bags of peanuts, and taffy apples, and filling glasses full of lemonade. He kept on taking in the nickels, too, and hoping he was counting the change right.

He was passing fifteen cents in change down to a white-haired man in the middle of the top row of seats when, from behind him again, came Colonel Castle's announcement:

"Now, ladies and gentlemen, you are about to witness those youthful equestrians *extraordinaire—Mademoiselle* Jeanette and *Monsieur* Ajax with their famous educated steeds!"

Again there sounded a roll of drums.

Toby was glad he had worked his way to the top row of seats. He had to turn around, even Harry Tupper would have had to admit. He had to come back down, too, as there was no other direction in which to go. And in coming back down, he couldn't help seeing Jeanette and Ajax make their imposing entrance!

On two beautiful snow-white horses they came, standing up and holding hands. To the strains of a Strauss waltz the horses cantered round the ring, white tails streaming behind them like banners.

How like a fairy princess Jeanette looked in her short ballerina skirt, pink and white and frothy. And how handsome Ajax looked, Toby had to admit.

Murmurs of admiration went up from the crowd at sight of those fresh-faced youngsters and their handsome mounts.

How many of the boys and girls now watching would go straight home after the show and try out the same thing on patient old plow horses?

Carefully Toby made his way down the space between the tiers of seats. He didn't cry his wares now. If anyone tugged at his sleeve and asked for something he saw to it that they got it. But—well, his tray was almost empty anyway and his pocket was heavy with coins he had received. He had done well already, or so he thought, and besides he couldn't take his eyes off the boy and girl in the center ring.

After one trip around the ring, Ajax stood on his head on the horse's back. Jeanette did the same. Around the ring they went again, in this position, rising to a handstand, and then standing first on one hand and then on the other.

It was a wonder they didn't slip off. But the circus folk didn't worry. They knew the backs of the horses were broad and had been liberally sprinkled with resin so the youngsters wouldn't slip. That was why the circus people called such horses "resin backs."

Someone did tug at Toby's sleeve and ask for a sack of peanuts. His eyes still on the ring, where Ajax had just turned a somersault on the back of his horse and Jeanette was preparing to do the same, Toby passed the peanuts down to the demanding customer. He received his payment and without taking his eyes off the daring young riders, he pocketed the coin. It felt like a nickel.

He paused then on one of the steps. No sense in hurrying. He had only one bag of peanuts left and two taffy apples and the pitcher was completely empty. But he did have to be careful of the empty glasses he had received back from his customers on his way down. Somehow he was pretty sure that the cost of any broken ones would come out of his dollar Saturday night!

Two roustabouts ran out into the ring with obstacles. The horses leaped right over them as though they had not been there at all. Then the men brought out huge hoops which they held in the paths of the white horses. The mounts, with riders now standing up, rose and leaped through the hoops, gracefully and seemingly without any effort at all.

While the horses and their riders were again cantering

around the ring, the roustabouts set fire to the hoops which were wrapped with material that burned easily and with a hot and searing flame. Around the hoops the flames spread until both were great circles of red tongues leaping upward.

On toward the flaming hoops came the horses and their daring riders.

A gasp went up from the crowd. How brave could those children be? Jeanette and Ajax were still standing on the backs of the horses, apparently as unconcerned as though they were riding in a buggy.

The horses reached the flaming hoops, again lifted themselves into the air, and sailed through them! Both horses and children landed on the other side without a sign of having been in mortal danger.

They were even smiling, and then they were bowing, for the applause was loud and deafening.

Toby started to applaud, too, he was so carried away by the wonderful act. As he did so the tray tilted and the pitcher started sliding off. A watchful customer, fearful of having it fall on him, caught it and set it back in its rightful spot. Toby smiled his thanks.

7 MR. STUBBS

Toby stood beside the stand watching Mr. Tupper count the money he had just handed to him.

"... thirty-five, forty ... sixty, sixty-five ...." Tupper handled each coin with extreme care.

The performance of the afternoon was over. The circus grounds looked as though a vengeful hurricane had swept through them. Empty popcorn and peanut sacks, intermingled with the wooden sticks that had once held taffy apples and spun sugar candy, lay everywhere. Peanut shells crunched underfoot. Roustabouts were doing a halfhearted job of clearing up some of it. But their enthusiasm for the task was low. They knew the same thing would be repeated that evening.

"I sold every glass," Toby said proudly.

Preoccupied with his counting, Tupper merely nodded.

Suddenly a scowl swept across his almost-pleased face. The kid really had done an outstanding job, selling and keeping track of the number of sacks and glasses and accounting for the money he received. He had always counted on his other helpers coming up short a nickel or a dime, though *he* never did. Tupper, however, had no intention of telling Toby what he thought. It would only serve to make the kid feel too important and, worse still, might make him ask for a bigger wage!

Tupper held up what looked like a coin. But he had known the instant he had seen it what it really was. Of all the stupid—"What's this?" he growled. "Why, you blithering greenhorn! Don't you know any better than to take a lead slug?"

Toby looked dismayed and felt guilty. That slug must have been given to him while he was intent on watching the show and he had only felt of the coins before putting them into his pocket. He would have to be more careful about that in the future.

"I'm sorry, Mr. Tupper," he said remorsefully. "I don't know much about money."

But he knew it was a weak excuse, that he could have told the difference between a real nickel and a lead slug!

Tupper stopped counting. He turned on Toby an extremely unpleasant look.

"Then I'll teach you," he said grimly. "Lesson number one: I'm replacing this slug with a nickel out of your first week's pay."

"Yes, sir," Toby answered meekly.

Somehow he had known that was coming. Uncle Daniel had once told him, jokingly, not to take any wooden nickels. Well, from now on he would be sure he took no more slugs!

Then Toby remembered something. He held out one hand, in the palm of which lay three good nickels. "And what do I do with *these* nickels?"

Tupper stared at the coins in the boy's hand.

"Where did you get them?" he asked suspiciously.

Toby shrugged and he, too, looked down at the money in his hand as though surprised it was there.

"They were left over," he said. He raised blue eyes again to Mr. Tupper. "When I tried to give them back to the customers they said, 'Keep the change.' "

Tupper, startled at this display of innocence, leaned against the edge of the counter to keep himself upright. But he made a rapid recovery, and, assuming an air of worldliness, he said, "That, my lad, is what—in circus parlance—we call a 'tip.' " He leaned forward and added in the voice of one generously sharing a great fund of knowledge, "As a matter of custom, all tips belong to the head concessionaire, which is me."

Tupper drew himself up grandly.

"Yes, sir," said Toby, crestfallen.

"However," Tupper went on with a magnanimous gesture, "if you report *all* your tips I'll split them with you. Thus—the dime for me, the nickel for you."

Overwhelmed by such generosity, Toby beamed, "Thank you, sir."

Tupper squinted at him.

"Remember," he cautioned softly, "you promise to keep our little arrangement secret. In the circus world one must pretend to have a hard nature. I shouldn't want people to think me a softy."

Toby regarded him gravely. Were all circus people like Ben Cotter, hard on the outside and soft inside? Still, Sam Treat didn't seem that way.

Tupper silently studied his young helper for a moment. He was almost unable to believe the stroke of good fortune that had come to him. Then, as though determining to take advantage of a good thing while he had it, he waved a hand toward a small mountain of glasses, bowls, crocks, and pitchers that were piled helter-skelter behind the counter.

"Now, get busy and clean up that mess," he ordered.

"Yes, sir."

Toby looked at the pile of dishes and gave a deep sigh. He didn't like washing them any better than anyone else would. Somehow there was no fun in that task. Uncle Daniel had often said that a person had to earn his own way in this world and, right then and there, Toby knew the old man had been right. He squared his shoulders and tackled the job at hand with as much enthusiasm as he could muster.

Tupper dug a battered old enamel dishpan from his living quarters behind the stand. He also brought out a badly dented bucket.

Bucket in hand Toby went toward an old covered well that stood on the edge of the circus grounds.

With a pleased smile on his face Tupper watched Toby go. Then he lit up a big cigar and drifted away.

Toby reached the well. Once a house had stood in this meadow but it had burned down, leaving the well in good condition. This was lucky for the circus folks. A source of water could often be a problem to them when they struck tents.

Toby let the well bucket down into the rock-lined opening, windlass flying around. He listened until he heard it hit the water below. He waited for it to fill and then he grasped the handle of the windlass and began to turn.

Up came the bucket full of water, up and over the side of the well. Toby poured its contents into the dented bucket he had brought. Then back to the stand he went, being careful not to slosh any more of the water onto his feet than he could help.

Once back he set the bucket of water on a charcoal stove to heat.

When the water steamed Toby tied the strings of an apron about his waist and poured some of the hot water into the dishpan over a generous portion of strong, soft soap that he found in Tupper's untidy tent. Then he started to work.

Arms elbow deep in suds he washed and washed. Carefully he rinsed the glasses in what was left of the hot water and polished them until they shone. Then he arranged them in neat rows on top of the counter.

The glass pitchers received the same treatment. After several more trips to the well, the crockery and pans, in which the taffy was made and the apples dipped and the spun sugar candy cooked, were washed and ready to be used again. It was hard work and Toby sighed with relief when, at last, he poured out the dishwater and rinsed out the pan.

Drying his hands he untied the strings of the apron and stepped off a few feet to look with satisfaction at the result of all his efforts. A big grin broke across his freckled face. Helping in the kitchen at home had taught him how to do this kind of work. The stand looked as neat as Aunt Olive's kitchen!

His eye drifted to several unsold taffy apples that sat on one end of the counter. Surely he had earned one of those. He walked over and scanned them closely. He picked out the biggest one, with the thickest coat of taffy.

Blissfully he nibbled at it, savoring the sweetness of both candy and fruit.

From somewhere nearby came a tremulous animal sound. Toby turned around and faced a row of animal wagons that had been parked just off the midway. From between the bars of the monkey wagon peered his chimpanzee friend, the one who had stolen his banana and thrown twigs at him. Colonel Castle's pet! Phooey! Colonel Castle could have him and welcome.

As though reading his thoughts the chimp let out another sound, more piteous than the previous one. The wizened face of the animal looked drawn, sad, and hungry as he cast pleading eyes at the boy eating the taffy apple.

Inwardly Toby chuckled. That chimp wasn't fooling him this time with those phony histrionics. No sir! Toby held the apple up, temptingly, and shot the chimp a big grin. With loud, smacking noises he nibbled at the edge of the bite he had taken before.

The chimp let out a wail, louder and more heart-rending than anything he had done before. As though in sheerest agony he grasped the bars of the cage and shook them.

What a ham!

Toby went over to the counter of Tupper's stand and carefully picked out two of the smallest peanuts on the display rack. Walking with a deliberately slow saunter, he carried them over to the monkey wagon. The chimp fixed a soulful eye on him and watched his every move.

Toby leaned against the side of the cage where the small monkeys were housed. He wasn't getting close to that canny chimp's part of the cage to give him a chance to snatch those two peanuts he was now holding up and rolling around in his fingers.

"Well," he said softly, "we're a little more friendly today, aren't we?"

He sent a twinkling glance toward the chimp. Whereupon the chimp returned a pleading one, at the same time making noises of impatience.

Toby squinted at the chimp.

"Know who you put me in mind of?" he asked, taking a nibble of his apple and smacking his lips again. "Old Mr. Stubbs who runs the general store back home."

The chimp snuffed. He hadn't any idea who Mr. Stubbs was, nor did he care. But the sight of Toby eating that taffy apple was more than he could bear.

"Yes, sir," Toby repeated, "the real bug-spittin' image of Mr. Stubbs. Hi, Mr. Stubbs!"

Toby waved the apple at Mr. Stubbs. Mr. Stubbs eyed the candy-covered fruit covetously.

Toby saw the look and read it correctly.

"No, sir. No, indeed," he said reprovingly. "But I tell

you what. You want to make friends, I'll give you this big, fat peanut. All right, Mr. Stubbs?"

The chimp made a noise in his throat that could have meant several things.

Toby nodded as though satisfied.

"All right?" he asked. "Gentlemen's agreement—that's the most solemn thing there is."

He tried to sound and act just like Mr. Tupper. He put out his hand. The chimp cautiously reached out toward the proffered goober. Toby took the small paw and shook it with exaggerated solemnity.

"Now, we're friends," his voice was sober. "And here's the peanut."

Mr. Stubbs took the peanut. He drew it inside the cage and held it close to his beady eyes and looked it over very carefully. Then, with a sound of disgust, he threw it through the bars onto the ground.

"Hey!" Toby yelped. He went over to where the peanut lay and picked it up. Again he handed it through the bars to Mr. Stubbs.

Mr. Stubbs took it without enthusiasm and rolled it around in his paw and looked it over again. He made another snort of disgust and threw it through the bars. It narrowly missed the end of Toby's nose as it sailed by.

Toby snorted this time and shot the chimp a look loaded with annoyance. He could take just so much from that ornery critter. He bent over to pick up the nut a second time. He did not realize that he was holding the taffy apple dangerously close to the bars of the chimp's side of the cage. But the chimp did.

Toby straightened up, nut in hand.

"Look here! If you want us to be friends . . . ."

He glanced at the hand that had held his delicious apple. The stick was there—but the apple was gone! And there was Mr. Stubbs, back so far in his cage that Toby couldn't reach him, grinning wickedly and holding up the apple.

Fury exploded inside Toby. That thieving chimp! Would he never learn to leave him alone?

Toby thrust his arms through the bars of the cage and reached as far as he could. But Mr. Stubbs cannily kept far enough back so Toby could not touch him, even with the tip of a finger.

Frustrated, Toby yelled, "You! Give that back!" And, in his anger, he shook the cage bars a little.

Mr. Stubbs eyed him mischievously. The chimp then

bit into the apple, chewed slowly, smacked his own lips, and burst into raucous chimpanzee laughter.

Vowing never so much as to look at that chimp again, Toby turned and stalked away from the monkey wagon.

He kept that vow, too—until that evening when he was summoned to Sam Treat's tent. He felt sorry for the chimp then, something he had never thought possible.

Toby stood on one side of the clown's tent, eying the table in the center. There, stretched out on that table, was Mr. Stubbs! Sick!

Sam was looking down at the chimp, real concern on his kindly face. Every one of the eight dogs was looking out of his trunk, feeling the same way if one could judge from the looks on their canine faces.

Toby's boyish face was creased with worry. The chimp wasn't fooling this time. He just lay there whimpering.

Toby looked at Sam. "He's awful sick, isn't he?" he asked.

Sam shook his head.

"Don't look so good," the clown answered, "that's a fact."

Sam leaned over the chimp. For a moment Toby couldn't see Mr. Stubbs, but he could hear his whimper.

Toby's conscience began to bother him. It had been his fault, he told himself. He should have been more generous that afternoon and given Mr. Stubbs a piece of his apple. Then the chimp wouldn't have taken and eaten the whole thing, which was just too much for a chimp's delicate digestion. He shouldn't have teased Mr. Stubbs with those runty little peanuts either.

"My fault," Toby said contritely. "I shouldn't have let him get hold of that candied apple."

Sam turned toward Toby for a second. Then, stroking his chin, he looked back at the prone figure of Mr. Stubbs.

"Probably wasn't the apple," he said thoughtfully, "so much as all the junk he stuffed down before that. Let's see here."

Sam reached down toward Mr. Stubbs's throat. Then he started handing things to Toby.

"Skate key," he said, giving it to the startled boy. "Couple of penwipers. Piece of chalk. Half a yard of twine. McKinley campaign button . . . ."

No wonder Mr. Stubbs was sick. Toby had seen goats eat about anything they could find, but he had never thought that an animal as smart as Mr. Stubbs . . . .

Then he laughed in relief. Sam wasn't really taking

all that stuff from Mr. Stubbs's throat. He was pulling a
sleight-of-hand trick on him, just to make him feel better.

"Gosh!" Toby cried. "You scared me. For a minute,
I thought—"

Sam laughed and patted Toby on the shoulder.

"He'll be all right, I think," he said soothingly. "This
fellow is practically indestructible."

Mr. Stubbs groaned loudly. If this was all the sympathy he was going to get. . . .

Toby peered around Sam and down at the chimp. Was
he just fooling again? No, that couldn't be. Mr. Stubbs
really looked sick.

"Can you fix him up?" he asked anxiously.

Sam nodded. "Always have," he said.

With that the clown went over to a portable packing
case. From it he brought out an imposing-looking jug.

Clucking with satisfaction Sam brought the jug back
to where Toby stood. Holding the jug close to Toby's
face, he tapped the label with a forefinger.

Toby took a look. The label read CASTOR OIL, just as
plain as day.

"Old Reliable," Sam said.

Toby blanched. If there was anything he had against

Aunt Olive, it was her firm belief that the vile contents of this jug could cure anything! And to think that Sam Treat felt the same way. Toby's knees started buckling.

The dogs knew what was in that jug too. Quick as a wink each slammed down the top of his trunk case, right on top of himself.

Feebly Mr. Stubbs opened one eye. He saw the jug. The sight had an immediate and electrifying effect on him. He sat up straight and began a leap to the floor of the tent, determined to make his getaway. But his break for freedom did him no good. Though Toby's conscience was now working overtime, he helped Sam seize the little creature and hold him tightly down.

"Take a good grip," Sam directed. "I'll give him a couple of spoonfuls. . . ."

Toby looked worried as well as conscience-stricken. "I was hoping to make friends with him," he mumbled. "He'll never forgive me for this."

Sam made a sound of impatience. Apparently he had forgotten his own boyhood when this very same stuff had been poured, under protest, down him.

"Hang on," he said grimly. "Don't let him bite you!"

Toby hung on, but he turned his head away. He saw

the tops of the trunks open and, from each, a dog's head slowly emerge, sympathy in every eye for the miserable creature on the table.

Mr. Stubbs struggled violently. He clenched his teeth. But Sam poured two tablespoonfuls of the oil into his mouth anyway.

With the first spoonful Mr. Stubbs's eyes glazed over. With the second one the fight went completely out of him and he went limp on the table.

Toby gathered the little chimp into his arms. With real affection he looked down into the wizened face.

"Sure hate to put him back in his cage," he said.

Sam nodded understandingly. "Be a good idea to keep him warm tonight."

"Maybe he can sleep with me," Toby said hopefully.

"You better ask Ben," Sam answered. "The monks are his responsibility."

Toby nodded. As he did so, Mr. Stubbs opened his eyes, gazed reproachfully at him and then, with a feeble cry, buried his face in Toby's collar.

Toby looked down at Mr. Stubbs, wholeheartedly sympathetic. He left Sam's tent hugging the small body tightly to him.

8 "GOOD WITH A SHOOTIN' IRON!"

The line of swinging lanterns gleamed in the velvety blackness of the night as the circus wagons moved on to the next stop.

Toby drowsed on the seat of the monkey wagon. Mr. Stubbs, wrapped in a blanket, rested on his lap. Beside them, Ben Cotter was driving as usual.

Ben thoughtfully reached for his pipe. He searched in one pocket after another. No pipe. What happened to it? Ben scowled. He always kept it in the right-hand pocket of his jacket. Now it wasn't in any of them.

He sent a glance toward the nodding Toby. What was that chimp up to? He didn't look very sick right now, leaning back against the boy and turning something over in his hairy paw. Whatever it was, Mr. Stubbs sniffed of it and sneezed. Ben leaned over, squinting. Why, it was his pipe! Ben snorted angrily and snatched the pipe away from Mr. Stubbs. Wiping it on his sleeve he jammed it into his mouth. Grimly Ben filled it and lit it.

Toby roused at the sudden movement and looked sleepily up at Ben. Ben saw that, too, and, with the pipe clamped between his teeth, he said bitterly, "How I let you sweet-talk me into this I don't know! Colonel Castle's number one rule is: animals stay in cages where they belong!"

At which Toby looked down at Mr. Stubbs sitting docilely in his lap. He gave the chimp an affectionate hug.

"I sure appreciate it, Ben. He's lookin' better," he said indicating his little pal. "I bet he'll be his old self again in the morning."

Ben gave Mr. Stubbs an irritable look. "Won't that be nice?" he growled. Then he gave the reins a slap and lapsed back into gloomy silence.

The lights continued to bob through the darkened countryside as the caravan continued down the lonely country road.

Next morning, Mr. Stubbs, still cradled in Toby's arms, heard a loud popping sound. The chimp awakened, sat up, and looked around.

Toby was still sleeping soundly.

Ignoring the chimp, Ben leaned over and shook Toby. The boy's eyes popped open and then went shut again. Ben gave him another shake. Toby grunted and, lurching forward a bit, rubbed his eyes.

"What time is it?" he asked sleepily.

"Late," Ben grumbled. "The canvas wagon had a break-down during the night."

Toby shook his head, hard. Then he stretched and yawned loudly. Soon he had broken out of the cocoon of sleepiness that had been so securely wrapped around him. He looked around.

"Maybe I ought to find Mr. Tupper," he said. "He'll be looking for me."

Ben laid a restraining hand on his arm.

"Hold your seat," the big man said. "We're going to parade straight through Woodvale. We'll set up canvas afterward."

Toby sat up excitedly, his blue eyes sparkling.

"Gosh!" he cried. "I get to ride in the parade!"

Mr. Stubbs, who had been rudely jostled, looked up reproachfully.

Ben turned and opened a box behind the driver's seat.

From it he took a cap and jacket which he promptly put on. Though wrinkled, Toby could see it was a fancy jacket of blue serge with gold braid trim. The cap was red, round and flat on top, and had a bill. Gold braid trimmed it, too, and a cockade stuck up in front.

From the same box Ben drew another cap, like his but blue in color. This he tossed to Toby.

"Here," he said gruffly. "You want to be circus, *look* circus!"

Toby caught the cap and admiringly whirled it around on one finger. Then he settled it onto his thatch of red hair. Without a mirror he had to imagine how it looked on him. The picture he saw in his mind was a satisfying one. He grinned broadly and asked, "How about a hat for Mr. Stubbs?"

Ben sputtered, "Never mind that." He glowered at the chimp and added, "Whatever you do, just hang onto him!"

Toby was too excited to answer. He could tell they were approaching a small town. Houses were closer together and here and there a small store stood by the road.

To his ears came a pop, pop, popping sound.

Then came street signs and more houses and stores and the cracking and popping became louder than ever.

Mr. Stubbs put his paws to his ears and grimaced.

Suddenly Toby looked at Ben and cried, "Hey! I almost forgot! It's the Fourth of July! That's firecrackers!"

"Yeah," Ben growled, "the big cats *love* them!"

Woodvale was in a festive holiday mood. Red, white, and blue bunting hung across the fronts of the stores and banners reached from one side of the main street to the other. The townfolk had been gathering for more than an hour to be sure each had a good spot from which to watch the circus parade. Now the sidewalks were lined with smiling, happy faces, old and young, and an air of excitement prevailed.

Here and there exuberant children were setting off firecrackers and their yells intermingled with the barking of dogs.

Around the corner, onto the main street, came the circus parade and a murmur of expectation went up from the onlookers. First came the outriders, and then Colonel Castle riding his prancing horse and looking very dignified indeed.

The crowd pressed forward. Behind the line two small boys set off a string of firecrackers. As their wagon went

by, the loud popping set the big cats to pacing nervously back and forth in their cage.

Another firecracker went off, a large one that exploded like a cannon being fired.

A lion let out a roar.

This pleased the crowd, looking for thrills anyway. But the horses drawing the monkey wagon reared slightly and Ben had to check them with an iron hand on the reins.

Beside Ben, Toby sat proudly erect. A short time ago he had been one of a crowd lining the streets to watch the circus go by. Now he was part of the circus! It seemed too good to be true.

He kept a tight hold on Mr. Stubbs just as Ben had told him to do. Right now Mr. Stubbs was struggling to get out of the coat Toby had so carefully wrapped around him and to sit upright.

A loutish-looking boy stood behind the line of watchers. In his hand was a long string of firecrackers. Grinning, he lit one of them with a match and then tossed the whole string into the air. Exploding one after another, the firecrackers landed on top of the monkey wagon!

Mr. Stubbs shrilled excitedly. He tried to break loose

from Toby's grasp. His chattering as he struggled on the seat of the wagon with Toby, and the loud popping of the firecrackers on top of the wagon, set the other monkeys into violent commotion!

The furor instantly spread to the other animals in the parade. The elephants trumpeted in fright. Tails curving, the cats prowled about their cages. A tiger screamed and a panther howled. Horses reared and strained at their bits and nervously side-stepped. The restlessness increased with every popping firecracker.

The older folks in the crowd began to sense the true situation and looked questioningly at each other. But the boys and girls seemed to think it was part of the show and enjoyed it hugely.

Ben kept a Herculean grip on his team of horses. The chattering, screaming monkeys and the other restless animals made it a hard job.

Then another packet of firecrackers was thrown into the street in front of the wagon and began their pop-pop-popping.

The horses reared. Ben strained at the reins. Toby clung to Mr. Stubbs. In spite of his efforts, though, Toby felt his grip on the animal loosen.

Another firecracker exploded nearby and Mr. Stubbs gave a final effort and broke loose. In a flying leap he left the driver's seat and landed on the back of one of the horses! The horse reared and pitched and so did its companion in harness.

The team swerved into the curb and crashed heavily into one of Woodvale's light standards!

"Look out, Toby!" Ben yelled. "Jump!"

Ben gave Toby a push. Then he, too, jumped. Both landed clear of the wagon just before it swayed and crashed upon its side.

Colonel Castle rode up then, dismay written all over his handsome face. No wonder. The entire side frame had broken away as the wagon hit the standard. Mr. Stubbs was standing beside the broken cage, shrieking and chattering. It was apparent that he was telling the monkeys inside that now was their chance to escape!

They took Mr. Stubbs's advice. Before Toby or Ben could slam the frame back into place the monkeys were scattering in the crowd.

Toby started in pursuit of two of the monkeys. Ben, seeing the animals were loose anyway, was trying to un-hitch the panicky horses from the overturned wagon.

"What in tarnation's going on here?" Colonel Castle demanded angrily. "What happened?"

Ben, still struggling with the harness and horses, turned and answered, "Chimp was loose, Colonel. Got scared of the fireworks and riled up the horses."

Colonel Castle scowled down at him. "How'd the chimp get loose?"

Ben hesitated, but only for an instant. Then he shrugged, lowered his head, and tugged again at the harness. "My fault," he said. "He was riding up top with me."

Toby, hearing this, whirled around. Horrified surprise flicked across his face. Ben was taking the blame for something that had been entirely his own idea! Why?

Colonel Castle looked stern and unyielding.

"You know the rules, Ben," he said grimly. "You're through! See me after the show!"

The owner of the circus whirled his horse to where two roustabouts were standing agape at Ben's predicament.

"Let's go!" Castle shouted above the uproar. "Pick up those monks before they tear the town apart!"

By this time Toby had reached Colonel Castle's side. He grabbed the man's boot and tugged at it.

"It wasn't Ben's fault, sir!" he pleaded. "It was mine! Mr. Stubbs was sick. I was taking care of him!"

Colonel Castle did not even bother to look down at the heartsick boy. He simply turned and rode on up the line of the parade, calling out, "Oley! Omaha! Get after those monkeys!"

He pointed toward a store roof. Toby looked, too, and saw two of the smaller monkeys scampering gleefully up toward the peak of it.

He saw another one of the little simians lolling comfortably, and insolently, atop the slack of an awning over one of the store fronts. At the same time Toby saw the boy who had thrown the string of firecrackers on top of the monkey wagon throw another lighted one at the monkey on the awning.

Right over Toby's head the firecracker swished. The monkey, however, saw it coming. He reached out one tiny paw and caught it deftly. The monkey looked at the sputtering fuse, chattered, and tossed it right back at the boy who had thrown it!

The firecracker exploded at the loutish boy's feet. The boy howled indignantly, adding to the already uproarious confusion.

Served him right, Toby thought grimly.

Mr. Stubbs! Where was Mr. Stubbs?

Toby hadn't noticed in which direction his new friend had gone. He *had* to find him. Down the street Toby went, looking and calling, "Mr. Stubbs! Mr. Stubbs!"

He looked up. He saw a monkey perched atop the cornice of a two-story building. The monkey seemed to be enjoying the efforts of a group of circus acrobats to reach him. They were forming a pyramid beneath him, standing on each other's shoulders. Sam Treat was on top of the pyramid. The monkey prolonged his fun by creeping a little farther back each time the clown came near enough to touch him.

It wasn't Mr. Stubbs. So on Toby went through the crowd, calling, "Mr. Stubbs!"

Then he heard a sound like that of another exploding firecracker. Toby stopped in his tracks as the front door of an office just ahead flew open and a man ran out.

He saw the star on the man's shirt. It was the sheriff. The building was the city jail. But what was he running from?

There came another popping sound. It was definitely not a firecracker exploding. It was a pistol shot! Toby saw the bullet nick the door jamb just behind the sheriff!

"Look out!" Sheriff Keller yelled. "Take cover!"

Toby took cover. In doing so he looked through the door out of which the sheriff had just come so abruptly. He froze in his tracks. Inside that office, atop the roll-top desk, stood Mr. Stubbs, a smoking revolver in his hairy paw!

Mr. Stubbs was unconcernedly swinging the muzzle of that gun toward two terrified prisoners locked behind the bars of two small cells visible from the sidewalk.

Toby quaked in his squeaky brogans.

The sheriff had by now moved cautiously up to a window, at the same time violently gesturing to curious people to keep their distance.

"Keep down!" he ordered. "The monk's got my gun!"

He raised his head and looked through the window into the office from which he had been so unceremoniously ejected. Both he and Toby saw Mr. Stubbs swing around and squeeze the trigger of the gun he held.

Toby dropped and so did the sheriff. The slug sailed harmlessly over their heads and buried itself in a lamp post.

The sheriff turned his head and yelled toward a general

store on the other side of the street.

"Ed Willis!" he hollered. "Get me a rifle out of the store! Hurry!"

Toby saw a man rush into the store as he went toward the sheriff at the window. The sheriff impatiently waved him back.

"You, boy," the sheriff hissed. "Get out of here!"

Toby stopped for a second. But he resumed his course, creeping, and reached the sheriff's side at the same time Ed Willis did.

The sheriff grabbed the rifle from Willis's hand and whirled back to the window. Then, just as suddenly, he and Willis ducked down.

Toby, standing directly back of them now, could see Mr. Stubbs, still standing on the desk, inspecting the thing in his paw that made such a racket when he squeezed the little thing-a-ma-jig on it. Mr. Stubbs looked like he was going to squeeze the trigger again. But he didn't. He just kept looking wonderingly down at the crazy contraption!

The sheriff took this chance to raise the rifle toward the window.

Terrified now for Mr. Stubbs, Toby cried out pleadingly, "No! No! Please don't hurt him!"

The sheriff glared at him as though he thought the boy had taken leave of his senses.

"Look out, boy! I hate to do this, but I'm going to get him before he shoots some innocent bystander."

Toby was beside himself with horror.

"Mr. Stubbs won't hurt anyone," he cried tearfully. "No!"

But the sheriff turned resolutely back to the window. He lifted the barrel of the rifle and aimed it at the chimp on his desk. Toby ran toward the jail door.

Into the jail he went and he headed fearlessly toward Mr. Stubbs. Mr. Stubbs heard him, turned, and aimed the muzzle of the pistol straight at the boy. The prisoners in the cells ducked when they saw the pistol aimed into the room again.

Toby saw that muzzle aimed right at him. He paused for a second and gulped.

"Oh, hi, Mr. Stubbs!" he said softly, trying not to let the tremor in his voice show. "It's me, Toby."

Mr. Stubbs waved the gun at him.

Cautiously Toby moved toward the chimp. "We're friends now, remember?" he coaxed. "Careful with that gun . . . careful. . . ."

Toby went forward two more steps. He could feel the eyes of the two prisoners on him. He knew the sheriff and Ed Willis were watching, too, in helpless fury. The sheriff couldn't shoot now for fear of shooting Toby.

Courage welled up even stronger in Toby. On he went, closer and closer.

"Good old boy . . . easy, Mr. Stubbs," he purred. "Easy."

Mr. Stubbs's beady little eyes never left Toby. He just stood there and watched the boy draw nearer, seemingly wondering what all the fuss was about. Suddenly he looked at the weapon in his hand and thrust it toward Toby.

Toby flinched. Suppose Mr. Stubbs just accidentally did squeeze that trigger! He'd be a goner, that's what. Still, it was worth taking another chance on. Might as well, anyway, now he had come this far.

Toby held out his hand and went forward a couple more steps.

"Here we go," he whispered.

Gingerly he took hold of the pistol in Mr. Stubbs's hand and took it away from the chimp!

Toby almost collapsed in relief. So did the prisoners

and the sheriff and Ed Willis. Mr. Stubbs just looked sheepish.

The chimp put his hand in Toby's and looked up at the boy in an obvious bid for sympathy.

"Too late now to be sorry," Toby scolded. "Come on."

Mr. Stubbs jumped down from the desk. Meekly he walked out of the sheriff's office, right past the two limp-looking prisoners.

Sheriff Keller and Ed Willis and several other people were clustered just outside the door. They watched Toby and Mr. Stubbs come out, hand in hand.

Toby handed the gun to Sheriff Keller.

"I guess this is yours," he said politely.

The crowd opened a path for him and Mr. Stubbs. The crowd, now that the tension was broken, laughed.

Sheriff Keller went back into his office. Toby heard a derisive voice cry out, "Hey, Sheriff—that monk's pretty good with a shootin' iron. Maybe you ought to deputize him!"

9 OLD SOFTY

That evening two roustabouts were making their way toward the monkey wagon. One, a tall, thin man, was carrying a squirming monkey. The other fellow, short and fat, had a chimp by the hand.

"That's the last of them!" said the short, fat roustabout as he started to shove the chimp into the side of the cage in which Mr. Stubbs was lounging.

"Hold it, Oley!" came the voice of Ben Cotter.

The strong man of the circus strode up to the side of the wagon he had driven for so long.

"That second chimp goes in with the monks," he added authoritatively.

Both roustabouts turned. They took in Ben's unaccustomed attire. Obviously dressed in his very best, and uncomfortable in the tight-fitting suit and high celluloid collar, Ben was carrying an old straw suitcase.

The roustabouts had known Ben was leaving. But somehow they hadn't expected this. They shrugged. So long as Ben was on the circus grounds he was boss of the monkey wagon. So the short, fat man took the second chimp away from Mr. Stubbs's quarters and shoved him into the side with the monkeys.

Ben watched the operation. Then he walked up to the side of the cage and looked in. It wasn't easy to say good-by to these monkeys and chimps. Even though they were a troublesome bunch, he had taken care of them for a long time and had grown to love them. To him their welfare was of real concern. But he made certain that nothing of what he was feeling inside at the moment showed on his face.

He turned to the tall, thin roustabout and said gruffly, "Remember, these ain't elephants. Keep 'em out of drafts. See that their straw is dry. And look out for that little one with the squinty eye. I think he's coming down with something."

"We'll look out for 'em."

And they would. Ben knew them well enough to be sure of it.

"See that you do," he growled.

Ben stood for a moment longer, watching the monkeys. If it hadn't been for that new kid he wouldn't be in this spot right now. He never should have let the redhead talk him into keeping Colonel Castle's pet chimp on top of the wagon last night, not even if the little animal was sick. He could have handled those horses, kept them in the street, if the chimp hadn't jumped onto their backs. It had been his fault all right. He didn't blame the colonel. Rules were rules and had to be obeyed in a circus as well as anywhere else.

Ben shrugged. It was like he had always maintained. It just didn't pay to be a softy, to kids, or animals, or anything else. From now on he would be tough, really tough. Then nobody could take advantage of him.

Slowly he turned away from the cage.

"Be seein' you, Ben," said the tall, thin roustabout, his voice full of sympathy.

Ben looked at him coldly.

"Sure." And he walked away without a backward glance.

Colonel Castle's white wagon stood across the circus grounds from the monkey wagon. With long, purposeful strides Ben started toward it. He would get this business over with in a hurry and get out of here—the sooner the better. He just hoped he didn't get any more sympathetic words or looks from anybody. He didn't need them and he didn't want them.

Why was Sam Treat coming this way? Fervently Ben hoped that Sam wasn't coming to say good-by. If there was anything Ben disliked, it was sad and sympathetic good-bys.

Sam fell into step beside him.

Ben looked at him suspiciously.

"Where are you going?" Ben swung his suitcase a little more vigorously than he had been doing.

Sam shrugged.

"Just out for a walk," he answered calmly. He looked up at Ben and raised an eyebrow. "Free country, isn't it?"

Ben turned toward Sam and lowered his dark, heavy brows belligerently.

"I know you, Sam," he growled. He jutted out a jaw, leaned over, and ordered, "Don't go puttin' your oar in with the colonel. I been trying to get away from this stickwhittle circus for years. Now," his stride lengthened as though he couldn't reach the owner's white wagon fast enough, "by sweet thunder, this time I'm going to do it!"

Sam nodded as though he knew exactly how Ben felt, had even felt that way himself at times.

"Sure you are," he said, as though firmly in accord.

Ben swung his suitcase over to the other hand, though anyone could tell it wasn't heavy. Ben didn't believe in owning a lot of clothes; just a change was enough for him.

Ben raised his chin, which even right after shaving, was bluish in color. He said stubbornly, "I'm gonna get a livery stable, make myself halfway rich, and laugh myself sick at all you sawdust soldiers!"

Sam clucked his tongue.

"Fine with me," he said. He pointed down the midway. "Go ahead! Go!"

Sam quickened his step then, too, so as to get Ben to the white wagon sooner and thus help him on his way to that bright future with as much dispatch as possible.

They reached Colonel Castle's wagon and rounded a corner of it. On the side where the door opened out Ben saw Toby waiting.

Inwardly the big man groaned. The kid was there to tell him, no doubt, that he was sorry he had caused Ben to lose his job and to say a sad farewell. And it was just the thing Ben had longed to avoid. It was the reason why he had picked this time of evening to take leave of the place, when everybody would be busy getting ready for the late performance.

Now, if the kid started to cry. . . . Ben knew how Toby felt. He knew that Toby felt responsible for Colonel Castle's having fired him. But there was no need for the kid to feel that way. Ben had convinced himself it was what he wanted anyhow—to get away from the circus. To get kicked out, he was also convinced, was the only way that would ever happen. So the kid could save his tears until such time as they might be needed.

Ben made sure that the scowl on his face deepened and darkened. But if Toby saw the scowl he gave no sign. The instant he saw Ben and Sam, the boy ran up to Ben and looked up at him with pleading blue eyes.

"Ben . . ." he faltered.

Ben turned his scowl on the boy then, full force. Pressing his lips together in a thin line of determination not to show any weak emotions, he stalked past Toby and started up the steps of the white wagon. On the top step he knocked.

From inside came the voice of Colonel Castle. "Come in! Come in!"

Ben opened the door and walked into the wagon.

As his friend disappeared inside, tears welled up in Toby's eyes. Ben had been gruff to him, but he had also been kind. And now the big man was losing his job because of him and Mr. Stubbs.

Toby felt Sam's arm about his shoulders, felt the gentle squeeze. Misery written all over his freckled face, he looked up at the circus clown.

"Why don't Ben tell Mr. Castle it was my fault?" he asked, a lump in his throat.

Sam looked down at Toby, a glint in his kindly eyes.

"Know why Ben's so big?" he asked. "That's mule-head pride he's stuffed with."

Sam gave Toby's shoulder a pat as though to add there wasn't anything anybody could do about a fault such as that, and Toby shouldn't take it so hard.

Ben found Colonel Castle inside the wagon at his desk, carefully counting a thick stack of currency. The owner of the circus did not look up as Ben walked in, but kept on with his job, slowly and methodically, his lips moving with his counting. The last bill counted he lightly tapped the edge of the stack on the top of his desk to straighten it. Then, deliberately searching through the contents of a small tin catchall on his desk, he came up with a rubber band. He snapped the band about the bills and put them into a tin box which he placed in a small safe back of his swivel chair. Then, and only then, did he look toward the doorway where he had known all along Ben was standing.

A jovial smile broke over the colonel's handsome face as his eyes rested on the big man awkwardly standing there, his hat in one hand and the straw suitcase in the other.

"Well," beamed Colonel Castle, "it's been quite a day! Those runaway monks fiascoed us into the best business we've had all season!" Exuberant as a small boy with a new red wagon, he snatched a paper off his desk and waved it at Ben. "Telegram from our advance man in Kingsville says they're sold out of 'blues' for the show there tomorrow!"

Fine, fine, thought Ben. First time in a long time that the 'blues,' or general admission tickets, had been sold out before the show hit a town. He shifted impatiently from one foot to the other. But what had that to do with him? He was through with the outfit!

Ben was glad to see the boss so happy about the coming run in Kingsville and its promised success. Usually Castle was worried about what was going to happen to them next, or how he was going to meet the payroll after a week of stormy weather when there hadn't been enough paid admissions to cover the cost of the food for the animals.

Ben stood silent as Castle read the telegram.

" 'Monkeys capture Woodvale!' " he chuckled. " 'Animals celebrate Independence Day by making break for freedom! Boy disarms gun-toting chimpanzee!' "

Ben grinned in spite of himself. Everybody in the circus had had a good laugh over Mr. Stubbs's chasing the sheriff out of his own office. Though, at the same time, they realized how serious the situation could have been except for the bravery and quick thinking of Toby. Ben felt a warm glow at the thought of Toby. There was a good kid, Ben knew that now, and he wished Toby well.

Some of the circus folks had laughingly suggested that perhaps Jesse James would be a more appropriate handle for such a desperate character as Mr. Stubbs. This almost brought another smile to Ben's face. That Stubbs was a character all right, with his cunning, mischievous ways!

Then Ben grew grim again. Stubbs was also the reason why he was here right now.

Colonel Castle tossed the paper back onto his desk. He beamed at Ben. "That busted wagon was the best thing that ever happened to us."

Then he seemed to notice, for the first time, that Ben was all dressed up in his Sunday best and was carrying a straw suitcase that most likely held his everyday clothes.

"Why the getup?" Castle demanded with a laugh. "You trying to scare the animals?"

Ben drew himself up to his full height and came within an inch of hitting the ceiling of the wagon. With great dignity, he replied, "I come to pick up my pay, Colonel."

A puzzled frown passed briefly over Colonel Castle's face.

"Pay?" He stroked his chin thoughtfully. "What for?"

Ben's face did not change expression. "You fired me today," he said.

A broad smile broke over Castle's features. He got up from his desk and walked over to Ben. He laid a hand on the big man's arm and said, as soothingly as though to a hurt child, "Now, now, Ben, you know me. I was just letting off a little steam. What's the good of running my own show if I can't get sore at people now and then?"

Ben kept right on staring straight ahead.

"If you'll just give me the money that's my rightful due. . . ."

Castle looked up at Ben then and spoke as to a spoiled brat. "Stop whimpering about your money! Where's that boy, Tyler?"

Now what? thought Ben. Had somebody got through to Castle with the story of the sick chimp and Toby playing nursemaid to it last night? Sam Treat, most likely. Why couldn't that infernal clown mind his own business for a change?

"Toby?" Ben said. "He's outside." He jerked his head toward the door of the wagon. "What's he got to do with it?"

Colonel Castle ignored the belligerent tone of the strong man's voice. He brushed past Ben, went to the door of the wagon, and sticking his gray head through it, he called out, "Toby! Toby Tyler! Come in here!"

Toby heard the imperious command. He and Sam hadn't budged an inch from their stand outside the wagon door.

Toby looked questioningly at Sam. What should he do?

Should he just tell Colonel Castle that Ben had been in no way to blame for Mr. Stubbs's riding on top of the wagon? Toby squared his shoulders. That was just what he would do. Resolutely he walked up the steps of the owner's wagon and through the door.

With one swift glance Toby took in the luxurious interior of the specially built wagon. His eyes popped when he saw the gleaming paneled walls, the thick carpet on the floor, the rich draperies at the tiny windows, and the shining desk. He missed nothing. Oh, to be the owner of a circus and live in such splendor!

The colonel's voice brought him down out of the clouds.

"Now, Toby," Castle was saying briskly. "I want you and the chimpanzee to ride up on the monkey cage tomorrow. People in Kingsville will want to look you over after those stories today."

Puzzled, Toby looked from Colonel Castle to Ben.

"Are you out of your mind, Colonel?" Ben asked angrily. "A chimp up on the seat? That's just how that whole fracas got started this morning!"

Ben looked at Colonel Castle as though wondering if the circus owner had lost his mind.

Castle, however, seemed indifferent to Ben's opinion.

"Ben," he said smoothly, looking the big fellow in the eye as closely as a shorter man could, "with you in charge I'm not worried about a thing."

So that was it, Ben thought—hornswoggling him into staying with the outfit! He backed away a few steps, his face a study in grim determination.

"Oh, no," he cried, waving a big hand in a huge arc, "no, *sir!* You don't get around me that way!"

His protestations fell on deaf ears. Castle turned Ben and Toby around and headed them gently toward the door, just as though everything had been amicably settled. As he did so, he looked down at Toby and said, smiling, "Toby, I'd like to thank you for saving that chimp's life today. He's kind of a pet of mine. I guess I got a weakness for troublemakers." He gave Ben a pat on a broad shoulder. "That's why I like old Ben here."

Toby was in a complete daze. If the colonel meant what Toby thought he meant, then Ben wasn't fired at all. The big man was going to keep on driving the monkey wagon and he, Toby Tyler, was going to ride up top with him during the parades, holding Mr. Stubbs!

It was hard to believe that things could change so quickly, like sudden sunshine after a drenching shower.

But Toby guessed they had.

Still Ben was protesting, "Colonel. . . ."

Why couldn't Ben leave well enough alone? Toby wondered anxiously. Why did he keep on arguing with Colonel Castle?

The colonel, however, was paying no attention to Ben. Instead, he patted Toby on one shoulder and went on, "Seems like you handled that chimp pretty well. How'd you like to take care of him? Keep him out of mischief?"

Toby's eyes were big and round as he looked up at Colonel Castle. He guessed he wasn't dreaming. The colonel looked real enough!

"You mean it, sir?" Toby managed to gasp out in his mounting excitement.

Castle nodded, his face extremely serious.

"He's your responsibility."

Toby's face grew as radiant as a star.

"Boy!" he breathed.

But Ben was far from radiant. His scowl was darker than ever, his brows fairly quivering with indignation. He was being shanghaied into this, that was what was happening. And after having planned his future so nicely, the livery stable, the quiet, ordered, peaceful life. . . .

"Look, Colonel—" he said.

Colonel Castle could stand no more nonsense. He took on his best, tough boss-of-the-outfit look.

"What are you standing around here for?" he bellowed. He shot Ben a withering stare. "Climb out of that banker's suit and get those wagons moving! It's a long haul to Kingsville!"

Sam Treat still stood outside the wagon. Overhearing this last remark, he grinned broadly. But he wiped the grin away the instant Ben and Toby emerged from the wagon. Wouldn't be smart to let Ben know that he had expected this to happen. Ben liked to have everybody think he was a very tough guy. Well, let the fellow think so, though actually he had never fooled anybody.

Sam allowed himself a very small smile as he took Ben's suitcase away from him. He winked at Toby, who was so happy he could hardly stand it, and said, "Welcome, Ben."

Ben's disgust with himself for not sticking to his guns showed all over. An old softy, that was all he was. He gave an irritated snort. Well, nobody was going to find out about it, not if he could help it!

10 TOBY IN TROUBLE

Two weeks later Toby and Mr. Stubbs walked along the deserted midway, carrying a bucket of water between them. Toby was really carrying the weight of the burden. Mr. Stubbs's paw just rested lightly on the handle.

Toby felt like an old circus hand this morning as he and his little friend made their way toward the popcorn, peanut, and lemonade stand. He had lots of work to do. Business had been brisk the evening before and it had been late when the last customers had left the grounds. Toby had been so tired he had fallen into his bunk and gone to sleep, leaving the dishes and glasses and crockery to wash up later.

That was this morning. Toby sighed and vowed he would clean up every night from now on, no matter how tired he was.

This was Saturday. Weatherwise it promised to be a perfect circus day, hot and sunny. Besides washing up dishes from the evening before, there were many preparations to make for the rush of business that would come with the afternoon performance—popcorn to pop, peanuts to roast and sack, and all those apples to dip in taffy. It made Toby tired to think of it.

Mr. Stubbs wasn't tired. He just skipped along beside Toby, pursing his lips and emitting something that might have been a chimpanzee whistle.

They neared the stand. Mr. Tupper was there, all decked out in a violently colored silk shirt with armbands. He was a sharp dresser, Toby thought, so different from Ben. The concessionaire was standing before a mirror fastened to a pole. Very carefully he combed his hair so the bald spot wouldn't show so much. He clapped on a straw hat and adjusted it to what he considered the right rakish angle. He looked himself over with satisfaction. Then, turning, he saw Toby and Mr. Stubbs and scowled.

"Come on, stop dawdling," he said sharply. "I've got to go into town on business. You remember everything I told you?"

Toby carefully set the bucket of water down on the

ground. He didn't want to spill any more than he could help, for the more he spilled the more trips he would have to make for more. It was going to take a lot of water, anyway, to wash up that mountain of dishes!

He looked up at Mr. Tupper.

"Yes, sir," he answered politely. He ran off his orders of the morning. "See that the stock is all locked in the green box. Fetch enough water for all the jars."

More water, whew! But he knew they would have to have quite a bit on hand with which to make fresh lemonade as they ran out.

He added, with emphasis, "And it's Saturday." And he stuck out his hand.

Tupper put on his best puzzled look.

"Saturday?" he asked, a lilt at the end of the word.

Toby eyed him unflinchingly.

"Yes, sir. The day you pay me."

Tupper gave him a reproachful look as he turned and opened the cashbox. He took out some coins. Lightly he shook them up and down in his closed fingers.

"And what, my young Croesus," he asked tartly, "are you going to do with all the money I been showering down on you the last couple of weeks?"

Toby kept his hand out and palm open.

"I save it, sir," he said.

Resignedly Tupper counted the coins and dropped them into Toby's hand.

Toby watched as they hit his palm. One, he noticed, looked peculiar, grayish and smooth. He picked it up and looked at it a little closer. Then he handed it back.

"That's a slug, Mr. Tupper," he said matter-of-factly.

Tupper lifted a surprised eyebrow. As though he couldn't imagine how it got there, he looked closely at the offending disc.

"So it is," he said, lightly flipping the slug. Then he laughed, a trifle forced. "Just wanted to see if you were on your toes."

Tupper handed Toby another coin, put the slug back into the cashbox, and closed the metal lid. He put the box under one arm, stole another look at himself in the mirror, adjusted the straw hat again, and started off.

Toby watched Tupper out of sight. Then he relaxed a little. Somehow the work around the stand seemed easier and went faster when Mr. Tupper wasn't around watching every move he made.

Toby winked at Mr. Stubbs and opened the front of

his shirt. From it he pulled a little pouch with a drawstring closing. He opened it, and with loving deliberation,
dropped the coins into it.

He thrust the opened pouch in front of the chimp's
face.

"You ever see so much money, Mr. Stubbs?" he asked
proudly. "Three dollars and forty-seven cents! I'm pretty
near rich."

Mr. Stubbs snorted irreverently and reached his hand
into the pouch. Toby hastily pushed him away. He
closed his eyes and dreamily asked, "Won't Uncle Daniel
be surprised when I bring all this home to him?"

He wondered then, briefly, if Aunt Olive had received
the note he had painstakingly written all by himself, addressed as best he could, and given to Mr. Tupper to
mail. In it he had tried to say he was well and with the
circus, and that he would be home again some day.

Still dreaming, he put the pouch away. Then he poured
the water from his bucket into the dishpan and set the
pan on the portable stove to heat. Turning to his companion, and giving the empty bucket a swing, he said,
"Well, we need more water. Keep an eye on the stand,
will you, Mr. Stubbs?"

Without waiting for an answer, he took Mr. Stubbs by the hand and led him a safe distance from the stock of unpopped corn and unroasted peanuts. There he tied the chimp to a pole.

"From over here," Toby grinned.

Mr. Stubbs had raided the green peanuts once since Toby had been here and the results had been disastrous.

Bucket in hand, Toby started for more water. Silently he wondered how many trips he would have to make before he would have the stand shipshape again.

Down the midway he went, toward a pump that provided the circus with water.

He approached the big top. The entrance was deserted now, but how it would come to life this afternoon! Just another evidence of the magic of a circus.

A couple of the side panels of the big tent were roped up to let air into the stuffy interior. Through the openings Toby could hear the rhythmic sound of horses' hoofs drumming on tanbark. Now and then the drumming was broken by the crack of a whip.

Someone, Toby knew, was practicing his routine in there, as was the custom when the tent was empty. Performers practiced as often as they could so as to keep their acts up to par and to improve them. Toby idly wondered who was working out now.

Never before had he stopped and looked inside while practice sessions were going on. He was always too busy and, besides, some of the performers wanted no audience while they might be trying out new routines.

Just this once, however, Toby's curiosity got the best of him. He peeked through one of the openings.

For a second he squinted, until his eyes became accustomed to the darkened interior of the tent. When he could see clearly he opened them wide.

There, in the center ring, were *Mademoiselle* Jeanette and *Monsieur* Ajax working out with their resin backs.

Dressed in practice clothes, Jeanette was on the back of Bingo, her favorite mount. She had confided in Toby once that Bingo was the best-trained of any horse she had ever ridden.

Around Jeanette's waist was a "mechanic," a strap and rope contraption that kept her from falling while practicing. A roustabout handled the end of the rope of the mechanic. It was strung from the strap around the girl's waist up through a pulley above, and down. The pulley pivoted around as horse and rider circled the ring.

Toby knew he shouldn't be there watching. He should be busy with his own work at the stand. Reluctantly, he started to move away from his vantage point by the entrance. At this instant, Jeanette caught sight of him and waved.

"Hello! Come in!" she called, smiling at him in a warm, friendly way.

It was evident then that she didn't mind an audience. So Toby forgot all about his own work and went inside the tent.

Ajax turned and saw Toby and scowled. Uncertain now of his welcome, Toby proceeded cautiously.

Jeanette dropped lightly from her horse and took a step toward Toby. So did Ajax. Toby eyed the boy rider warily.

Ajax made no effort to hide his contempt for the bashful, awkward Toby.

"Well, if it isn't the great peanut salesman," he sneered. "The death-defying daredevil of the lemonade stand. . . ."

Toby winced.

"Stop it, Ajax!" Jeanette said sharply. Looking straight at Toby she added sweetly, "We haven't seen you around much lately."

Toby grinned bashfully. He shifted his empty bucket nervously. Around Jeanette he felt as awkward as an elephant, and much more dumb. He wished he could be as poised and sure of himself as Ajax.

"Well," he gulped at last, "I haven't had much time. Mr. Tupper kind of keeps me going."

Ajax wrinkled his nose in disdain.

"Sure," he said derisively, "he's got important business— chasing the flies away from the lemonade."

Ajax let out a loud and raucous laugh at his own wit. Toby flushed to the roots of his red hair.

Jeanette did not think the taunts were funny. She flashed an angry look at her smirking partner and unfastened the strap of the mechanic around her waist. She shoved the leather belt into Ajax's hand, at the same time smiling at the new boy. "Don't mind him, Toby."

Toby's usual happy, cheerful grin flashed across his freckled face. Not even Ajax and his barbs could keep his naturally bubbling spirits down for long.

"Oh, I don't mind him," he said, adding mischievously, "Next to Mr. Tupper, he's kind of friendly."

Jeanette laughed, a tinkling sound. Ajax scowled. The young equestrian didn't like being bested at anything, particularly by one he considered an ignorant hayseed.

Something very soft and velvety rubbed Toby's shoulder, then his cheek. Toby turned to see Bingo's head beside his and he couldn't have been more pleased. Next to chimps, he loved horses best.

Bingo nuzzled his ear. Toby gently stroked Bingo's nose. Jeanette looked pleased. Ajax looked even more unfriendly. Right now, Toby didn't care.

"Sure is a pretty horse," he said, rubbing his own cheek against the horse's jaw.

Jeanette looked misty eyed. "You like horses?" she asked softly.

Ajax snorted. "What would a peanut seller know about horses?" he asked loftily. "Come on, Jeanette, let's get back to work. Watch this!"

Fastening the mechanic around his own waist, Ajax turned and ran lightly across the ring toward his resin back cantering around. With a graceful, flying leap the young rider landed atop the moving horse. It was a trick that took a great deal of skill and courage and Toby knew it.

Toby watched enviously as Ajax rode past him and Jeanette. Ajax wore a smirking, satisfied expression that

Toby would have wiped off if he could.

Toby turned to Jeanette and said defensively, "I *do* know something about horses." His chest expanded. "It so happens I got a horse of my own."

He was stretching the truth and he knew it. But he had to do something to make a big impression on Jeanette!

Jeanette looked surprised.

"Toby! Really!" she exclaimed.

Dismay filled Toby for an instant. Had he started something he couldn't stop?

"Name's Old Red," he gulped, adding quickly, "Course, he's not really old. That's just his name."

Jeanette clasped her hands in front of her and her eyes shone warmly on Toby.

"I think that's just marvelous!" she cried with enthusiasm.

It was all Toby needed. He really started launching his little boat of exaggeration.

"Old Red's just about the best horse in the country," he went on, surprised at his own audacity. "Regular fire-eater. His father was a cavalry horse at Fort Donald. Fought Indians, maybe."

Jeanette listened, beaming. "Is he a gaited horse?"

Toby was taken aback by the question.

"Gaited?" he asked in confusion.

"You know," Jeanette said in a voice that implied he must. "What gait does he favor most?"

A feeling of relief flooded Toby. Why hadn't she said that in the first place? He answered brightly, "I think he favors the gate most that opens down to the pasture." He winked. "Lots of sweet clover there."

Jeanette's hearty laughter could be heard around the tent.

"Oh, Toby," she cried, "you're joking."

Toby beamed. He had made a big impression on her and he couldn't have been more pleased.

It didn't please Ajax. Standing up straight on his cantering horse, he passed them, scowling. Suddenly he called out, "Jeanette! Look!"

At the imperious command Jeanette turned toward the ring. So did Toby. They saw Ajax doing a shoulderstand on the back of the moving horse.

Admiration rose in Toby. You had to hand it to that Ajax! "Gosh, that's pretty good!" he said.

Jeanette wrinkled her turned-up nose and turned away. "Don't look at him," she said. "He thinks whenever he's out in that ring, the whole world has to stop and watch him."

Toby had to keep on watching. It just seemed he couldn't help it. He saw Ajax make a graceful recovery from the shoulderstand and could see how pleased the young equestrian was with this show of his skill. Toby also saw how angry Ajax was that Jeanette was deliberately looking the other way.

"Tell me some more about Old Red," Jeanette said, her face still turned away from the ring. "Can he jump?"

Toby whirled. "Can he jump?" he cried. "Like the time he saw a copperhead coiled up in a potato furrow!"

Jeanette looked confused.

"Furrow?" she asked.

Unknown to them, Ajax, growing angrier by the second at their inattention, was unstrapping the leather safety belt from about his waist. They heard him, though, when he yelled, "Hey! Jeanette!"

Jeanette turned impatiently. So did Toby. They were just in time to see Ajax hold up the belt and toss it aside with a flourish. Jeanette gasped.

"Ajax!" she cried in horror. "You know what the colonel says about working without the belt."

Ajax laughed contemptuously. "Aw! Who needs that thing! Watch!"

Drawing himself up, Ajax crossed his arms on his chest and posed there, cockily, as the horse circled the ring. Then he gave a dramatic flourish and cried out, "Now that I have your kind attention, I should like to perform the most hazardous of all feats — a genuine, forward somerset!"

Toby could hear Jeanette draw in a deep breath.

"Ajax!" she cried. Toby knew then that this was something Ajax hadn't tried before, at least not without the mechanic to help him perfect it.

Ajax paid no attention to Jeanette. He began balancing himself in preparation for the stunt. The roustabout who had held the rope of the mechanic came forward, a look of alarm on his rugged face.

"Cinch!" cried Ajax. And he poised himself for the beginning of the leap.

Toby saw Sam Treat come into the tent. If the stunt was as dangerous as Jeanette seemed to think, Toby hoped the circus clown would stop it in time.

Sam tried, but couldn't stop Ajax. The young rider, seeing the clown coming toward him with a restraining hand upraised, curled his lip confidently and launched himself forward.

Ajax's slim body flipped over. But, instead of landing on the broad rump of the horse as he had expected to, Ajax hit it a glancing blow. Jeanette screamed as the boy slid off and crashed heavily to the floor of the ring.

Toby, Jeanette, Sam, and the roustabout rushed toward Ajax, writhing on the ground. One foot was twisted painfully beneath him.

Toby reached his side first. He tried to lift Ajax so the pressure would be off the foot. Ajax shook him off, saying angrily, "Get away from me!"

Ben Cotter came into the tent then, and another roustabout, and Colonel Castle.

Colonel Castle hurried over to where Sam Treat was bending over the injured boy. Sam looked up at the colonel and said softly, "Pretty bad. . . ."

Toby looked down at Ajax, sympathy written all over his freckled face. This was a tough break for the young equestrian and Toby felt genuinely sorry for him.

Colonel Castle looked down at Ajax. Then he turned to one of the roustabouts and said briskly, "Get a stretcher! Move! Send for the doctor in town!"

Brusquely he asked of the others, "Who's responsible for this anyway? Who let this boy practice without a mechanic? Ben? Where were you?"

Ben's brows beetled angrily and Toby didn't blame him. The only one to blame for Ajax's condition was Ajax himself. But the boy rider kept silent while he was being gently lifted and put on a stretcher and carried out of the tent.

Colonel Castle watched the moving operation. Then he went on, "Never mind! Never mind! Don't bother me with it now! Question is—now what? Here we are going into our peak playing time, and now a top act goes up the chimney!" His sharp gray eyes played over the group. "What do we do about it?"

Jeanette spoke up.

"Colonel?" she asked.

Colonel Castle turned fondly toward her.

"What?"

"Toby Tyler can ride."

Colonel Castle blinked.

"Who?" he asked, as though he had never heard the name before. Ben turned and stared at the girl, as incredulous as the colonel.

"Who?" the strong man queried.

Toby was more surprised than either of the men. He couldn't believe he was hearing right!

Jeanette answered earnestly. "It's true. Toby's been riding since he was little. He has his own horse at home."

Toby picked up his bucket. He'd better get out of here before things really got out of hand. He started toward the entrance of the tent.

He had taken about two steps when he was stopped in his tracks.

"You!" Colonel Castle bellowed. *"Boy!"*

Toby turned, his eyes rounded in innocence. "Sorry, sir," he said hastily. "I'll get right back to the lemonade stand."

The penetrating gray eyes of the owner of the circus swept critically over him.

"Can you ride?" he asked in a no-nonsense tone.

Toby glanced at Jeanette, almost reproachfully.

"Me? Well—" he stammered helplessly, "it was just around the farm . . . kind of."

Castle waved impatiently.

"Never mind that. Just so you have *some* experience. I'll take care of the rest!"

Ben saw Toby's confusion and panic and correctly guessed the cause of it.

"But, sir," he began. "I don't think—"

"That's good!" Castle snapped. "Don't think! Now, stand there next to Jeanette. Let's see what we've got here. . . ."

Toby obeyed uncertainly. Colonel Castle walked around him and Jeanette, sizing them up. Critical, at first, his expression began to soften. Then he smiled at the youngsters warmly.

"Sure. *Sure!*" he beamed. "They jibe together like ham and beans. Whaddye think, Ben?"

"Now hold on, Colonel—" Ben protested.

Colonel Castle brushed him off as he would a fly.

"Yes, sir, we may have something here if we work at it right," he enthused. "That right, Sam?"

Sam Treat grinned. He had worked for the colonel so long he knew him like a well-thumbed book. The man had an uncanny way of sizing things up right. Sam nodded.

But Ben—he was so disgusted he could not hide his feelings. He scowled at Sam. Why did that clown always agree with Colonel Castle?

Colonel Castle took Toby by the lapel of his jacket and held him firmly.

"Now, you listen to me, Toby What's-Your-Name. Let's get this straight," he said sternly. "We're going to make a bareback rider out of you. It won't be easy. But, by the eternal, that's exactly what's going to happen! Understand?"

Toby gulped and protested, "But, sir, I've got to work for Mr. Tupper. We—we've got a gentlemen's agreement."

Colonel Castle snorted, "I'll take care of Tupper."

Then he whirled to the others and went on, "Ben, start first thing in the morning. We'll be at the county seat in Waterford in two weeks. I want this boy riding by then. Now, take over. He's all yours!"

Turning, the owner strode off confidently, as though certain everything had been settled satisfactorily.

Ben called after him, "Colonel!" The big man sounded worried. "Two weeks? Be reasonable!"

He might as well have been addressing the wind for all the response he got. Castle had disappeared through the entrance of the tent before Ben was through protesting.

Sam grinned at Ben's discomfiture, but not for long.

Ben settled that with an angry glare at the clown.

Sam said, "Well, I've got to be going. Zee you lader."

He started to leave, but found it impossible. Ben had stepped on one of his feet and pinned it to the floor.

"You heard the colonel," Ben growled. "He's all ours."

Sam knew he was hooked. He joined Ben in looking speculatively at Toby. Toby looked apologetically at them. He knew that, while he might have made a big impression on Jeanette, he certainly hadn't on Ben and the clown.

11 DEAR THIEF!

"It's not fair, Colonel," Tupper said unhappily. "Toby Tyler's the best boy I ever had. You can't take him away from me."

It was later the same day. Harry Tupper had just been summoned to Colonel Castle's white wagon and told the news—that Toby was to be trained to be a bareback rider!

Castle threw an impatient look at the dismayed concessionaire.

"Will you stop whimpering and get out of here!" Castle exploded. "Find yourself another boy."

"I don't want another one," Tupper retorted imploringly. "Customers like him. He brings in a lot of tips— uh—I mean money."

"Listen, Tupper. . . ." The colonel's tone was ominous.

But Harry Tupper was not a person who gave up easily. He tried another tack.

"Now, Colonel," he wheedled, "don't go boilin' up. I know you're a hard man. People say lots of things about you, but I never heard no one say you weren't fair and honest."

Castle's brows lowered.

"Don't you try to bear-grease me," he growled.

Castle had had dealings with Tupper before. He knew all his bag of tricks. But Tupper kept on trying.

"I feel responsible for that boy." Tupper sighed heavily. "He's liable to get hurt fooling around them horses."

Castle sat down at his desk. He opened a drawer and took out some papers.

"Ben will take good care of him," he muttered without looking up. "You know that."

Tupper took a step forward. He twisted his face into what he thought was an expression of real concern.

"Colonel, it just don't rest easy on my conscience," he whined.

Colonel Castle looked up and squinted.

"Just how much do you think it would take," he asked sarcastically, "to soothe that conscience of yours down?"

Triumph flickered in Tupper's mean little eyes.

"Well, I hate to put it in terms of money," he answered softly, "but I'd say, oh, about forty dollars a week?"

He might as well ask for more than he expected to get, Tupper silently reasoned. That way he might get closer to what he really hoped for.

Thoughtfully Castle thumbed through several of the papers. He picked out one of them and held it in front of him and studied it.

"I figure the going rate on your conscience," he said, his eyes still on the paper, "a lot lower than that." He looked up sharply. "Suppose we make it ten."

Tupper leaned over the desk. Shrewdly he asked, "How does thirty sound to you?"

Castle yanked open another drawer.

"It sounds like fifteen," he said, taking out another sheaf of papers.

Tupper leaned forward a little farther.

"Colonel, I'd like to help you." His manner was as oily as the spots on his fancy vest. "Tell you what I'll do. . . ."

Colonel Castle controlled, with great effort, the anger and disgust that surged up within him. Was there no limit to this man's cheek? He looked up at Tupper's fawning face and gritted, "No, Mr. Tupper, I'll tell you what *I'll* do! You get twenty dollars a week finder's fee for that boy, and if you say another word about it—"

Castle half rose, menacingly.

Tupper jerked back, smiling weakly.

"That's a fair proposition, Colonel," he said hastily. "I'll just draw up a piece of paper, legal-like. . . ."

"You'll *what?*" Castle thrust his face close to Tupper's.

Tupper took a step backward. The colonel was getting riled now. He had best let well enough alone.

"We'll just make it a gentlemen's agreement," he said expansively. He held out a hand invitingly. "After all, if we didn't trust one another, what kind of world would it be?"

Castle pointed toward the door of his wagon.

"Get out!" he exploded.

Tupper beat a hasty retreat.

"Yes, Colonel!"

The door banged shut behind him.

Toby was giving things some serious thought that night. He sat atop the monkey wagon, Mr. Stubbs cradled in his arms. It was one thing to be a concession-aire in a circus, but it was something entirely different to be an equestrian. Colonel Castle expected a lot of him. Could he live up to those expectations? He couldn't blame the colonel for expecting so much. After all he had told Jeanette . . . Toby shuddered at what he had told her!

Ben sat beside him, silent, puffing on his pipe. The big man seemed lost in thought, too.

Toby gave Ben a sidelong glance.

"Ben—" he began.

Ben took his pipe from his mouth and looked at it. "Yeah?"

Toby took a deep breath. Somehow he had to summon the courage for what he had to do.

"You ever tell a lie?" he asked, staring straight ahead into the darkness. It was easier to talk to Ben like this, when he didn't have to face him.

Ben cleared his throat. "Same as anyone else," he grunted. "I finally gave it up. Too much trouble."

Toby gave the big man another sidelong glance.

Ben went on, "Any lame brain can lie hisself into something. Then there's all that trouble of working yourself back out of it. Not worth it."

Toby sat silent for a moment as he and his friend stared straight ahead. Mr. Stubbs stirred faintly and changed position in Toby's arms.

"Ben," Toby said softly. "I told one of those lies."

"Don't say?"

"I can't ride. Not hardly at all."

"I know it."

Toby looked at Ben. Ben blew out more smoke. He watched it disappear into the night air.

"When you figure on leaving?" Ben asked quietly.

Toby's eyes widened. Could Ben read his thoughts?

"How'd you know?" he asked.

Ben shrugged. He added in a sort of offhand way, "Ought to be a pretty good pile of coins in that pouch by now."

Toby fingered the pouch that hung on a cord about his neck.

Ben turned toward Toby and said, with studied unconcern, "I guess you could buy a train ticket home, and still have enough money to give your Uncle Daniel."

Toby straightened up.

"You don't think I'm a quitter, do you, Ben?" he asked stiffly.

Ben took another puff on his pipe. He eyed the boy beside him.

"Depends," he drawled. "Some people belong in a circus. Some don't."

Toby crumpled back into his former position.

"Ben?" he asked in a very small voice.

"Yeah?"

Toby swallowed the lump in his throat.

"Will you look out for Mr. Stubbs? He don't know I'm going."

Ben tapped the ashes out of his pipe. With great deliberation he put it into a pocket of his coat.

"He won't starve," he answered briefly.

Toby looked at Ben, wonderingly. How could the big man be so icy cold at a time like this? Didn't he ever feel anything? Didn't he ever get all choked up and teary inside?

Toby wished he could be calm and cool and unconcerned like Ben. It would be a lot easier to leave if he were. But he just wasn't built that way.

Toby looked down at the sleeping Mr. Stubbs. A big tear rolled down his cheek and splashed on top of the chimp's head.

"I'll come back some day," he said softly, "and buy him from Colonel Castle."

"Sure," Ben answered gruffly. "Why don't you get some sleep?"

Toby tried to stifle a sniffle and couldn't. He felt disgusted with himself. Holding onto Mr. Stubbs, he climbed over the back of the wagon seat and settled himself and the chimp on a pallet that lay on top of the monkey cage. Toby liked to sleep up there. It was always cool and the sway of the wagon soon lulled him into slumber. Of course, sometimes he rolled and hit the built-up sides, but he usually went right back to sleep again.

He lay down, but tonight sleep wouldn't come so quickly. He just stared at the stars overhead and kept right on thinking.

Then, being careful not to disturb Mr. Stubbs, he sat up straight.

"Ben," he said softly, "next to Mr. Stubbs you and Sam are the best friends I got. I'll sure hate to say good-by."

Ben didn't answer for a minute and Toby couldn't see the muscles of his jaw working.

"Don't get all wrought up," he answered finally, his

voice as cool and collected as ever. "Few weeks, you'll forget what I looked like."

Toby's eyes were on the back of Ben's head silhouetted against the moonlit night, the heavy, black hair topped with a checked cap, the thick neck and square shoulders.

"I'll never forget you, Ben," he said softly.

Ben's lips tightened as the muscles in his jaw quivered.

"Go to sleep," he said gruffly.

Toby sniffed again and lay back on the blanket on top of the pallet. Clasping his hands behind his head, he continued to look at the stars overhead, blurred now by the tears in his eyes. Mr. Stubbs stirred again and Toby covered him with a corner of the blanket. Mr. Stubbs snuggled against his side. A wave of affection for the chimp swept over the boy. He would miss Mr. Stubbs, and Ben, and Sam. He would miss them unbearably.

Still, he couldn't stay and let Jeanette and Colonel Castle catch him in a lie.

Why had he told them about riding Old Red in a way that had led them to believe he had done it bare-back style, that Old Red was his horse? They had taken it for granted that he had been around horses and ridden them all his life. The truth was, he had never really been close to a horse until he had gone to live with Aunt Olive and Uncle Daniel! And the only riding he had ever done was sitting firmly on the old horse's back and going to the pasture to round up the cows.

And Old Red! He was so slow you had to look twice to see if he was moving at all! A baby could ride him without falling off. The old plow horse was a far cry from being the prancing creature that Jeanette and Colonel Castle had apparently pictured him to be.

Toby closed his eyes and sighed. He had been so anxious to make a big impression on Jeanette. What would she think of him after he had left?

He rolled over flat on his stomach and buried his face in his arms. Why did life have to be so hard? In no time at all he was fast asleep.

Soon Ben's head was nodding. On the circus caravan moved, toward its destination.

Mr. Stubbs stirred and wakened. He sat up and scratched himself behind one ear. He looked down at Toby, fast asleep beside him. He uttered a small, questioning sound. The boy didn't move.

The chimp looked around him, as though wondering what to do with himself now that he wasn't sleepy anymore. He looked again at Toby. Then he seemed to remember something. A wide grin broke over his wizened face.

One hairy paw shot out quickly and slipped inside Toby's shirt. It drew out the pouch with the coins in it which was still attached to the string around Toby's neck. Mr. Stubbs pursed his lips. He set to work and untied the string. Toby never moved.

With the pouch resting on his knees, the chimp then loosened the drawstring. He looked in and saw the shining coins that the boy thought were so wonderful.

Mr. Stubbs picked one of the coins out of the pouch. He sniffed at it. He turned it over and over and intently studied both sides of it. He bit into it and made a face. Then he disgustedly flipped it over his shoulder. It made a little pinging sound as it hit a boulder beside the road!

Mr. Stubbs drew out another coin, apparently hoping for better luck. This he sniffed, looked at, bit into, and threw away!

Toby kept right on sleeping and Ben's head kept right on nodding.

Mr. Stubbs proceeded to toss one after another of the coins out into the night. Finally there were a half dozen or so of them left in the bag. These he contemptuously scooped up and threw out, all at once.

Still neither Toby nor Ben wakened. Mr. Stubbs peered into the pouch to see if anything else of interest to him might be lurking in it. It was empty. Disgusted he let the pouch drop beside Toby. Then he lay down on the far edge of the pallet and went back to sleep.

Next morning Toby was wakened by Ben calling up from the ground beside the wagon.

"Toby! Better get up! You got a big day ahead of you!"

Toby opened his eyes, stretched, and sat up. He saw that the caravan had pulled off beside the road. Not far away, through a grove of tall trees, he could see the waters of a small creek sparkling in the early morning sunlight.

He looked down at Mr. Stubbs, who had crept up close and was cuddled against his side. It was going to be hard. . . . He saw the pouch! Horror-stricken, he snatched it up and looked inside it.

Oh, no! Up on his knees, he looked wildly around the top of the wagon. Realization of what had happened hit him with the suddenness of a thunderbolt.

Toby turned blazing eyes on the chimp.

"Mr. Stubbs!" he cried in agony. "My money? Where is it?"

Roughly he grabbed Mr. Stubbs and shook him. The chimp, unused to such treatment, whimpered in fear.

Toby's face reddened with fury. He shook Mr. Stubbs again.

"What did you do with my money? Tell me!"

Then, realizing the futility of what he was doing, he let Mr. Stubbs go. He scrambled again around on top of the cage, looking, hoping. . . .

"What's the trouble?" Again Ben's voice came up from below.

Toby's distraught face appeared over the side of the cage wagon.

"Ben! Have you seen my money?" he cried. "It's gone!"

Ben looked up, incredulously.

"You sure?"

Ben dropped his eyes and began looking at the ground around the wagon.

Toby choked back a sob. "Mr. Stubbs had the bag!" he wailed. "He must have thrown all the money away!"

He sank hopelessly back on his heels.

"Why, the ornery, thieving little brute!" Ben exploded and he started threateningly up the side of the wagon toward Mr. Stubbs.

Mr. Stubbs drew back in terror. His beady little eyes rolled around searching for an avenue of escape. What had he done to make these ordinarily affectionate people so angry at him?

Ben climbed over onto the top of the wagon and began looking around too.

Toby leveled an accusing look at the cringing chimp.

"Mr. Stubbs, why did you do it?" he asked in despair. Mr. Stubbs moved close to him in an attempt to make up.

Roughly Toby pushed him away.

"Get away from me!" the boy cried bitterly. "I don't want you around anymore! Go on!"

Ben slowly turned toward Toby.

"Take it easy, Toby!" the big man said softly.

Locking his arms about his knees, Toby rocked miserably back and forth. He glared again at Mr. Stubbs.

"That's what I get for making a friend out of him!" he said. "Get away!"

Ben fixed Toby with a reproving look. Sternly he

said, "Near as I remember, Colonel Castle said he was your responsibility. You took him on, didn't you? Nobody made you do it."

Toby looked away and sniffed.

"No."

"Then don't go blaming the monk."

Toby's sigh ended with a half sob.

"But all my savings! My money is gone!"

"You think money's your only problem? That's easy!"

Ben pulled a wallet from his pocket. Opening it he pulled out several bills and handed them to Toby.

"Here—take what I've got. There's enough to get you home, and some left over."

Toby stared dully at the money. He made no move to take it.

Ben shook the money at him. "Go on!" the strong man said angrily. "Take it and get out of here before you get in any deeper."

Toby made no move.

Ben went on, "What's the matter with you? You mean you *don't* want to run away? You want to go on taking care of this ungrateful thieving little monk? You want to go out in the practice ring today and work off some of that trouble you lied yourself into?"

Toby's head drooped.

"All right," Ben said with finality. "See you're in that ring at eleven sharp this morning! And don't think it's going to be fun!"

Ben slammed down off the wagon.

Toby watched Ben go. With the sleeve of his jacket he wiped away his last tear. Then he reached out and drew Mr. Stubbs into his arms.

Toby kissed Mr. Stubbs on top of his head. Ornery, thieving little brute! How could Ben have said such a thing!

12 MONSIEUR TOBY

Later that morning Toby was trying his best to place his feet, hands, or some part of him on the back of the white horse cantering around the ring somewhere beneath him. He knew he looked pretty silly, hands and feet outstretched, flying around up there above the animal.

He was dressed in a pair of patched, cast-off tights that had once belonged to Ajax. The mechanic was fastened around his waist with the other end of a rope manned by Sam Treat. The outfit alone was enough to unnerve him. The leather belt of the mechanic bit into his ribs in an excruciating manner.

Sam was endeavoring to maneuver Toby so he would be directly above the horse. Toby, wearing a startled expression, circled the ring about a foot above, somehow unable to make any direct contact with the elusive beast.

Ben, whip in hand, stood in the center of the ring, in this, their first practice session.

"Go on!" Ben yelled unfeelingly. "Get on the horse! He won't eat you!"

Toby made a lunge downward with the upper part of his body and seized the harness. Desperately he tried to pull himself down to a sitting position on the back of the horse. He landed flat on his face, and around the ring he rode, bumpety, bump.

Tethered to one of the ring-side seats was Mr. Stubbs. The chimp watched dubiously. Judging from Toby's present performance, he seemed doubtful that Toby would ever make much of an equestrian.

Toby floundered to a sitting position. There! He would rest a bit and get his breath.

"Now!" yelled Ben. "Stand up!"

Startled, Toby turned toward the big man. Did he mean that? Yes, he did. Toby clenched his teeth. Slowly, and with great effort, he managed to get to his knees on the stand-up pad on the horse's back. Then, his arms flailing like windmills to keep his balance, he made it to his feet.

But not for long. In spite of his best efforts, his arms

went one way, his legs went the other, and off the rump of the horse he slid. There he was, dangling in the air, with the horse taking off a few feet ahead of him.

He was glad that Sam, at least, seemed to know what he was going through. The clown smiled sympathetically as he worked his end of the rope so Toby would be ready for the horse when it came around and under him again.

Around came the horse, closer and closer. Toby tried to steady himself, and Sam tried to help. Now . . . now!

The horse was directly beneath him. Sam let out the rope, ever so carefully, and maneuvered the pulley above. He would make it this time, Toby was sure of it. One toe touched the horse's back. Then, snap! went Ben's whip!

"Up!" bellowed Ben. "Take your place again! Up!"

Toby was startled. Trying frantically, he did land both feet on the horse's back, but well back on its rump.

"Now," Ben kept on, "on your feet! Bend your knees! Carry your weight low till you get the hang of it."

Toby tried to follow instructions, all the while feeling Ben's critical gaze upon him.

Then Jeanette came in, dressed for rehearsal, and stood

and watched. Toby had to do it right then. He had to show her that his story of being a rider had some truth in it.

He stood erect, for one brief triumphant moment. Jeanette seemed to share it with him. Then Toby faltered and toppled forward!

On the way down Toby grabbed the horse around the neck and held on with the desperation of a drowning man clinging to a straw. Opening his eyes he found himself staring into the animal's mouth!

"No! No! No!" yelled Ben. "Let go!"

Toby let go his strangle hold on the horse's neck. With Sam's help he scrambled back onto its back. But when he landed, he was facing one way and the horse was facing the other—and his nose was buried in the stand-up pad!

Toby lay there for an instant, hopelessness flooding through his battered body.

"It's no . . . use . . . Ben! I can't . . . do it!"

Slowly Ben turned, his eyes following the horse around the ring. Toby made no further effort to get up.

"That's just what *Monsieur* Ajax said would happen," Ben said grimly.

Toby's head jerked up from the pad. "Oh, he did, did he?" he sputtered.

Ben pursued his advantage. He yelled angrily at the redheaded boy lying prone on the horse's back.

"What he really said was, you'd put your tail between your legs and quit the first day!" Ben snapped his whip. "Ready? Let's try those mounts again."

Sam gently lifted Toby from the horse. With the mechanic he set the boy on his feet on a small ramp beside the ring. The horse went on its way around.

Toby waited grimly for the resin back to come abreast of the ramp. He'd show that Ajax that he was no quitter!

Nearer and nearer came the horse. When Toby thought it was close enough, he gave a mighty leap. He cannoned into the animal's side, and bounced away!

Back on the ramp, he waited for the horse to make another circle. He leaped again. This time he landed, successfully, on the back of the moving animal. Shakily he got to his feet.

Ben watched, grim satisfaction on his dark face. Sam smiled, pleased. Mr. Stubbs applauded noisily.

Monsieur Toby! It was going to be great!

A pleased smile played on the features of Harry

Tupper, watching through the open flap of the tent. Yes, sir, it was his lucky day when he met up with that redheaded Toby Tyler. None of his other boys had turned out, or paid off, half as well. He would see to it that nothing happened to put an end to this bit of good fortune.

He turned and left, not waiting to see Toby make three successful turns around the ring, on his feet.

"Good enough for a start," Ben said approvingly. "Few more turns and you can take a rest."

Toby left the tent some time later, feeling pretty pleased with himself. *Monsieur* Toby! Yes, sir, it was going to be wonderful being a performer in the circus!

A short distance down the midway one of the circus men was standing on a ticket podium in front of a tent. Gathered around him were a dozen or so performers and some roustabouts. On a packing box before him lay some packages and a stack of letters.

"Oley Matheson! Madame Tenzini!" the man called out.

Oley and Madame Tenzini came forward. The man handed a letter to each of them. Eagerly the recipients opened their mail and began to read. Mail was just as welcome to circus folks as to anyone else, sometimes more so, because all of them were away from home and loved ones.

"Here's two for you, Tony!"

Tony, a tall, thin, bearded roustabout stepped forward. He took his two letters. Some of the others, who hadn't received their mail yet, eyed him enviously.

Toby passed on by without stopping. He hadn't received a single letter from Aunt Olive or Uncle Daniel. He guessed they just didn't care much, as they must have received his note telling them where he was.

At first he had stood with the group waiting for the mail to be handed out. But not any more. Though he still hoped someday he would get one. It just seemed that watching too hard for something to happen always made it slower in happening.

Tupper was in the group, waiting and confident.

"Greta Neilson! Toby Tyler!"

Tupper looked quickly around. He was just in time to see Toby disappear into a dressing tent. Whew! That was close. He stepped up to the podium.

"Toby's busy now," he said engagingly. "I'll take it for him."

The man handed Tupper two letters that were addressed to Toby. Harry slipped them into his pocket and walked quickly away.

Tupper went straight to his lemonade stand. It wasn't at all neat this morning, without Toby to clean it.

Tupper went behind the counter. He looked carefully around to make sure no one was watching. Then he took the two letters from his pocket and studied them. Both were postmarked Guilford. He knew who had written them. Again he looked around. Then he took a penknife from his pocket and slit open one of the envelopes.

Tupper took out the sheet of paper inside, unfolded it, and began to read, half aloud, " 'I'm afraid your Uncle Daniel is not well. Without your help, the work around the farm is too much for him. We need you, Toby—' "

"Mr. Tupper!" Toby's voice sounded uncomfortably close.

Tupper started violently and the letters slid to the ground. Toby, dressed in a robe with a towel around his neck, ran to them and picked them up.

Harry Tupper held his breath. If Toby looked at the addresses on those envelopes, Tupper would be out the twenty dollar finding fee he was going to receive each week from Colonel Castle.

Toby, however, did not even glance at the envelopes. Politely he handed them back to the concessionaire.

Tupper snatched them and hastily put them into a side pocket of his coat. He smiled at Toby, a big, cordial smile, and this time it wasn't forced.

"Thanks," he said. Then, with a big wink, he asked, "Well, how is our star performer getting on?"

Toby looked rueful.

"Awful," he said with boyish frankness. "But Ben says to come back right after lunch."

Tupper patted him on the shoulder, a fatherly gesture to a son of whom he was proud.

"My boy," he said grandiosely, "I have complete faith in you. And just to prove Harry Tupper is not just sounding off his bazoo, look what I have for you."

Tupper stepped quickly behind the canvas curtain that separated his living quarters from the stand. He stooped and rummaged in the drawers of a carry-all. While Toby watched curiously, the concessionaire dug into the bottom. Triumphantly he came up with a pair of fairly new riding shoes!

Handing them to the surprised boy, he said proudly,
"The best secondhand riding shoes money can buy!
Now, is Harry Tupper your friend, or is he?"

Toby gulped and took the proffered shoes. A faint
look of remorse crossed his freckled face.

"Mr. Tupper—" he stammered.

Tupper waved his hand grandly, "There, there, boy,
don't thank me. Now just forget about your chores here.
Run along and see your friend, Mr. Stubbs."

Toby turned to go. Then he stopped and looked back
at his generous friend and said guiltily, "Mr. Tupper,
I don't know how to say this, but I want to take back
some of the things I thought about you."

Tupper was momentarily taken aback. Why, the ungrateful little wretch! After all he had done for him!
For a fleeting instant Tupper was tempted to take back
the shoes. Then, thinking better of it, he masked his
feelings.

"Think nothing of it," he said smoothly. "I admit
I'm not the most patient man in the world. But it's
how we behave when the chips are down that counts.
Am I right?"

Something akin to affection for Tupper rose in Toby.

Beneath that tough manner was a heart of gold, maybe, like Ben's. He nodded, too choked up to speak. Then he walked away.

A satisfied smirk on his face, Tupper watched him go. When Toby had disappeared around the corner of a tent, the concessionaire took the letters from his coat pocket, folded them carefully, and with a grim smile put them into an inner breast pocket. There they would be safe from the brat's prying eyes!

That evening, by the light of a lantern, Ben was busily shoeing one of the circus horses. In the tent near the lantern, lying flat on his stomach, Toby was trying to write by the flickering light.

Chewing on the end of a stubby pencil, Toby looked thoughtfully down at the writing tablet before him. Mr. Stubbs peeked over his shoulder to see how much the boy had accomplished and clucked with disgust at the still blank sheet.

Toby was trying to write a letter to Aunt Olive and Uncle Daniel, a real letter and not just a few lines telling where he was and that he was well. Most likely they hadn't received *that* one, anyway. He probably hadn't addressed it right and had misspelled most of the words. After all, he hadn't gone to school much and knew little about such things. There *had* to be some reason why he hadn't heard from them.

This time he would be more careful and get everything right. He looked up at Ben.

"How do you spell 'uncle'?" he asked.

Ben stopped his work. He looked uneasily over at the boy on the ground.

"Depends," he answered uncertainly. "Some parts of the country they spell it one way, other parts, they spell it the other."

Ben went back to his blacksmithing. Kids could ask the darndest questions!

"Why don't you write the letter to your aunt?" he asked impatiently. "Her bein' the female, it's politer. Easier to spell, too—*A-N-T*."

With that Ben picked up a large rasp and started working on the surface of the hoof to be shod. The horse looked around disapprovingly at such treatment.

Toby tapped a tooth with the end of the pencil.

"Trouble is," he said ruefully, "I never wrote a real letter before."

Ben shrugged. "Oh, it's more or less just like talking. You ask them, friendly like, how they are; tell them how *you* are; throw in something about the weather. . . ."

Bravely Toby started to write. A few seconds later he lifted his head and asked, "You think I could tell them about me learning to ride bareback all this time?"

Ben grinned at him. The kid was doing better at letter writing than he could have done himself.

"Guess so," he said. "Colonel Castle says you're coming on fine."

Toby, far from pleased, turned anxious eyes on Ben.

"What do *you* think, Ben?" he asked. To him the big man's approval meant more than that of Colonel Castle. "Could I be a good rider?"

It wasn't good, Ben reasoned, for a kid to get a swelled head. That Ajax was a good example of that. So Ben answered grudgingly, "Well, you ain't Pawnee Bill." He shrugged. "But I don't figure you're hopeless."

Toby wrote down all about his learning to ride, ending with, "I'm going to make you proud of me."

"That's the stuff." Ben beamed approvingly.

Toby kept on writing.

"I must close now—" he read aloud.

"Hold on!" Ben cried. He went on awkwardly, "First, say something about how you love them. Folks set a lot of store on things like that!"

Toby nodded. Good idea. He bent again to his task, biting his tongue with every curve of the pencil.

"I love you both a lot."

He wanted to write, "Cordially yours."

"*C-o.* . . ." He looked up at Ben for help. Ben fitted the shoe to the hoof of the horse.

"Just say, 'Your good friend, Toby Tyler,' " Ben firmly directed.

Disgustedly Ben realized that the shoe was too small for the hoof. With his bare hands he spread it until the ends were an inch farther apart. He tried it again and it fitted perfectly.

Toby smiled to himself and folded the letter. He put it into an envelope and, with Ben's "help," addressed it. Holding it up at arm's length, he regarded it with a great deal of satisfaction. It should reach its destination, tell Aunt Olive and Uncle Daniel how he really felt, and bring a speedy answer, he hoped.

Taking Mr. Stubbs by the hand, he left the tent with the sound of Ben's hammer ringing in his ears.

13 TUPPER'S PLAN

The show had started. The aerial act was on. Though Toby was in his dressing tent, he could tell by the lively number the band was playing.

Toby felt all thumbs. One big butterfly after another chased around inside his stomach.

This was the big night, the one he had looked forward to and dreaded. This was the night he was to make his debut as a bona fide performer in Colonel Castle's Great American Circus!

Mr. Stubbs was perched on the edge of a dressing table nearby. He watched the nervous Toby and chattered softly. Toby turned to him and frowned.

"Sure, I'm scared!" Toby told the chimp, his teeth chattering. "You would be, too, if you had to go out in front of all those people!"

Hands shaking he kept pulling on an old hand-me-down riding costume that had once belonged to *Monsieur* Ajax.

When he had it on, Toby looked at himself in a mirror. He snorted in disgust at his reflection. The outfit was at least six sizes too big for him; the sleeves came down and covered his hands and, as he saw when he turned around, the seat bagged ludicrously.

"How does it look?" he asked of Mr. Stubbs, as if he didn't know!

Mr. Stubbs put his paws over his eyes and made an unintelligible sound deep in his throat.

Toby tried to reef in some of the baggy rear. The results made him more disgusted than ever. Sam appeared in the door of the tent.

"How we getting on?" the clown asked cheerfully.

Toby shook his head. He took another turn before the mirror.

"It doesn't seem to fit very well," he said ruefully.

Sam looked him over, his eyes half-closed.

"Ledt's zee here. . . ."

Sam went behind Toby and tried to gather up some of the slack.

"Vee take zome of da schlack here," the clown said, "undt make da back to front . . . undt you zee, it's . . . you couldn't hardly ask for a . . . where else could you find . . . it's awful, isn't it?"

"I think so," Toby answered gloomily.

"Even magic couldn't help what it looks like," Sam commented, shaking his head. "Of course, there's the magic where you pull the rabbit oudt of—no! Then, there's the magic that—no, that's no good. Oh, ho! oh, ho! Do I know magic! Close the eyes! Close the eyes!"

Puzzled Toby closed his eyes. He could not see the broad grin that spread over the clown's face nor see him motion to someone just outside the tent.

"Ledt's zee now, how does that go?" Sam chuckled. " 'Needles undt pins; needles undt pins; when you presto the chango, the magic commences.' Open your eyes!"

Toby's eyes flew open. They widened even more when half a dozen other performers, including Jeanette, tripped into his tent.

"Surprise!" cried *Signorina* Zorelda.

"Good luck, Toby!" added Orcata.

"Congratulations," said Mr. Bogliostro, the tattooed man, and Professor Corbett.

Sam bowed. *"Monsieur* Toby," he began.

"Who?" Toby looked around, not quite accustomed to the new name.

"Monsieur Toby," Sam said again, with a grin that was wide and as pleased as could be, "this is a memorable occasion. In a few moments you will make your debut as a featured performer in Colonel Castle's Great American Circus!" Sam threw up one hand in a grandiloquent gesture, and the others clapped enthusiastically.

"But—" sputtered Toby.

Sam went on, "We, your fellow performers, not wishing to see the luster of this occasion dimmed in any way—particularly from a sartorial point of view—"

"Huh?" Toby was bewildered by the flow of big words.

Jeanette interrupted impatiently. "What he means is: You can't go out there wearing those baggy old tights!"

Sam nodded. "Exactly!" he cried. "Therefore, the aforesaid performers have joined forces and created for your kind approval—this handsome riding costume!"

Before Toby's amazed and delighted eyes, Jeanette unfolded a handsome red velvet equestrian costume! She held it out to Toby. Then Toby saw the ribbon, stretched

across the chest, on which was embroidered in gold thread: *Monsieur* Toby.

"On which I embroidered most of the name myself!" Jeanette added proudly.

"Gosh—I—" Toby stammered, dumbfounded.

"Please wear it," Sam said. "We wish you all the luck in the world."

Before Toby could realize his good fortune, or duck, Jeanette had leaned over and kissed him lightly on the cheek. The other ladies in the group followed suit. Then Sam motioned everybody out of the tent and started out himself.

Toby, speechless, watched them go.

In the entrance of the tent Sam turned and said, "You've got three minutes, *Monsieur* Toby."

Toby swung into action. As fast as he could, without putting his arms into the legs of his new costume, he scrambled into it. He stood again before the mirror. What a beautiful outfit! He admired himself in it. Wearing it he felt like a new person. He could go out there now and put on a fine performance. Clothes might not be able to make the man, but they could make a big difference in how he felt!

Jeanette and their two horses waited at the performers' entrance to the big top for Toby to appear. She frowned slightly. It was taking him a long time. Then she smiled at the thought that perhaps Toby, in his haste, had put the costume on backward and had had to change.

Over the center ring the aerial act was in progress. One flyer after another sailed from catcher to catcher through the air. Jeanette watched them for a moment with interest. Their sense of timing was uncanny. It had to be, in so dangerous an act.

Jeanette was glad she worked with a horse. If she slipped she didn't have nearly so far to fall!

The trapeze artists were going into their finale. Where was Toby? Surely he knew they were going on next.

Toby had put on his new costume and he knew he had it on right. Then he had looked down at his feet.

"My shoes!" he cried, looking around wildly. "Where are they?"

Mr. Stubbs scratched an ear, puzzled. He looked around, too.

Suddenly remembering, Toby clapped a hand to one side of his head.

"Good night!" he yelped in dismay. "I left them over

at the lemonade stand! Wait here, Mr. Stubbs!"

In his sock feet Toby made a dash out of the tent. He left behind an excited Mr. Stubbs who immediately started to pick at the tether that held him to a pole. He wanted to help Toby.

Jeanette kept on waiting, getting more worried and impatient by the second. She tried to keep one eye on the center ring and the other in the direction from which Toby should be coming.

From the ring strode Ben.

"Where's Toby?" he asked as he neared her.

"Still dressing, I guess." Jeanette tried to keep down her rising indignation. Was Toby going to spoil their first performance together by being late?

If she could have seen Toby then, racing frantically between the line of stake poles, she would have thought differently.

Mr. Stubbs succeeded in loosening his tether and dashed out after Toby.

The chimp ran right between the legs of Ben, who had just come to the entrance of the dressing tent and stuck his head inside.

"Toby!" he called sharply.

He saw that Toby wasn't in the tent. He turned and looked after the chimp. Something was wrong, Ben was sure of it. He started out after Mr. Stubbs and Toby.

Toby hurried toward the lemonade stand. He ran into the living quarters of Harry Tupper. He opened the drawers of the carry-all, looking for his shoes.

A moment later Mr. Stubbs came in.

Toby turned toward the chimp.

"Mr. Stubbs! How did you get loose?" he asked.

Mr. Stubbs's answer was gibberish. Then he started hunting, too, imitating Toby as best he could.

Toby found the shoes on the ground beside the carry-all. He sat down to put them on. He had to hurry. He and Jeanette were due in the center ring right now, most likely.

Mr. Stubbs hadn't found anything, so he kept on looking. He started pawing through Tupper's coat, which hung on a camp chair nearby. Mr. Stubbs stuck his nose into one pocket after another, sniffing disgustedly at their emptiness.

Toby was frantically trying to get a good tight knot in a shoe lace and keep an eye on Mr. Stubbs at the same time.

"No, Mr. Stubbs!" he cried out in annoyance. "Get away from there!"

At that moment Mr. Stubbs gave a triumphant cry. He had found something too! From one of the pockets he pulled several letters and spilled them on the ground.

Toby hurriedly started to pick them up. He was about to stuff them back into the coat pocket from which Mr. Stubbs had yanked them, when his eye fell on the name and address on one of the envelopes. He stopped short and stared at it in wide-eyed surprise.

" 'Master Toby Tyler,' " he read, " 'care of Colonel Castle's Great American Circus, Route—' "

His voice shaking, Toby read it again. " 'Master Toby Tyler!' " Excitement mounted high within him. He forgot everything but the letter he held in his hand. "It's from Aunt Olive!"

He flipped quickly through the other letters.

"They're *all* for me!" he cried in disbelief. Happiness flooded through him as, with shining eyes, he added, "Mr. Stubbs! They did write!"

Ben appeared at the flap of the tent's entrance. Angrily he strode in.

"What in thunderation are you doing here?" he

growled. "Come on!"

Toby looked up, his freckled face beaming.

"Ben," he said, happily thrusting the letters out so the strong man could see them. "Look! They did write!"

Ben snorted impatiently. "You don't have time for that now! Hurry!"

Toby remembered then, where he was and what he was supposed to be doing. Out of Tupper's living quarters he ran, toward the performers' entrance to the big top. Ben picked up Mr. Stubbs and hastily followed.

The music for the aerial act ended just as Toby skidded to a breathless stop beside Jeanette. She gave him a relieved smile and handed him the rein of his horse.

Colonel Castle's resonant voice came from inside the tent: "Now, ladies and gentlemen, we present for your kind approval those daring young equestrians—*Mademoiselle* Jeanette and *Monsieur* Toby!"

Into the tent swept Jeanette and Toby, leading their horses. They bowed deeply and gracefully, first to the right and then to the left. Loud applause greeted the handsome children so stunningly costumed.

Toby's cup of happiness was full and brimming over. For the first time since he had started training to become an equestrian, he felt he could succeed. So many people were depending on him to do a good job. They had all been so kind, even Aunt Olive and Uncle Daniel.

He looked out into the stands and saw the sea of faces and heard the clapping hands. The people out there expected him to do well too! He gathered all his forces together. At the flick of Jeanette's whip, he moved into his routine.

Standing on the backs of the horses, Jeanette and Toby cantered around the ring. Toby rode with all the confidence of a veteran performer.

Toby could feel Colonel Castle's eyes on him. Colonel Castle expected him to do a good job.

Roustabouts placed barriers on both sides of the ring. Up and over them the horses leaped, the young riders taking the jumps with ease and grace. The crowd applauded loudly.

Toby could almost feel Ben's glow of satisfaction as the strong man watched. Ben was depending on him.

The barriers were raised higher. Again Toby and Jeanette took them easily. The applause was louder than before.

Harry Tupper was watching, but Toby didn't see him.

Why had Tupper kept those letters? That thought went briefly through Toby's mind.

He and Jeanette went through the finale of their act, jumping through the flaming hoops! They rode out of the tent to resounding applause.

Passing through the performers' entrance, Toby and Jeanette smiled happily at each other.

A group of performers stood in front of the entrance. Frantically they waved for the young riders to go back into the big top.

The applause had not stopped. Instead it was rising to a crescendo! It was an ovation! They had done what every performer dreams of doing—they had stopped the show!

Around the ring they went again and did two of their routines again. Toby's spirits soared at the sound of the applause. He saw the pleased smiles of the other performers and Colonel Castle and Ben and Sam, and knew he had lived up to their expectations.

Then, on the way around the ring, he saw Harry Tupper. Harry was holding his hands above his head and clapping mightily so that Toby would be sure to see him.

Toby was glad that Tupper felt the way he did, and a little surprised. Some men in Tupper's position might have been angry because Toby had left and risen to a higher position in the circus world. But Tupper seemed pleased. It took a big-hearted man to feel like that.

The letters! They still puzzled Toby a bit, but he smiled at Tupper. Tupper smiled back thinking, "That boy's a gold mine."

Toby and Jeanette wheeled their horses around and rode back to the edge of the ring. The horses bowed and so did the riders. To the thunder of more applause they rode out of the tent.

This time the well-wishing performers opened a way for them. Toby and Jeanette slid off their horses and two grinning roustabouts came forward and took the animals and led them away.

"You were wonderful, Toby!" cried the Great Orcata.

"Excellent! A real trouper!" exclaimed Professor Corbett of the calliope.

"Great, boy! You rode like a veteran," beamed Mr. Donald Dinsmore, owner and trainer of the dancing elephants.

All the others nodded in agreement with the more

vocal of their group. They patted Toby on the shoulder and beamed at him.

Toby felt wonderful. It seemed no time at all since he had left Aunt Olive and Uncle Daniel and joined the circus, and here he was a full-fledged performer in it. If it hadn't been for Mr. Tupper and that free pass— he looked around for Mr. Tupper, but could not see him. Somehow he would show Mr. Tupper how much he appreciated all he had done for him.

The letters! Again they came back to him. After the well-wishers had drifted away, he hurried toward the dressing tent.

Inside the tent he found Mr. Stubbs, again tethered to the pole. But Toby paid no attention to the chimp as he sat down on a bench in front of the dressing table. From the inside of his riding costume he took those precious letters. He opened one of them and began to read.

Mr. Stubbs sat and watched. He wrinkled his nose and scratched an ear. Something was happening, he seemed to be thinking, that he could not understand.

Toby's eyes had misted over. Very softly he read, " 'We miss you so much, Toby, and wonder why you haven't answered our letters.'" Toby looked startled at this. He read on. "'I'm afraid your uncle is not well. He has taken over the chores you used to do, and together with the rest of the work, it's too much for him.'"

Toby looked up. He could see Uncle Daniel carrying armful after armful of wood for that wood box that, to him, had seemed to have no bottom. There was the old man driving the cows to pasture and bringing them home, with Old Nelly being ornery as usual and straying off. Then, too, he could see his uncle hoeing and weeding in Aunt Olive's garden, gathering eggs, mending fences—the thousand and one other things that had kept him, so much younger, hopping from early morning until dusk. And besides all that, walking behind the plow, hoeing the corn, and all the other work that had kept the old man so busy during the same waking hours. Taking care of the duties on a farm was a big job for a young man who was strong and healthy, but for one as crippled up with arthritis as Uncle Daniel. . . .

Unseeing, Toby's eyes wandered about the tent. They rested on Mr. Stubbs.

"They want me to come home, Mr. Stubbs," he said softly, his eyes glistening. "They need me."

Mr. Stubbs whimpered. But Toby had made up his mind. Quickly he got up and started taking off the beautiful costume his circus friends had given to him.

Very carefully he folded it and laid it on one of the rounded trunk tops. Just looking at it brought a lump to his throat. He stroked its soft folds. Never again would he wear anything nearly so splendid.

He had come so close to entering the world he had dreamed of when he had lived with Aunt Olive and Uncle Daniel. Now he had to give it all up. It wasn't easy.

But Aunt Olive and Uncle Daniel had depended on his help around the farm more than he had realized. Colonel Castle could get another boy to ride in the ring with *Mademoiselle* Jeanette. And Ben and Sam? They could get along without him better than the old folks could.

"I've got to go," Toby told Mr. Stubbs, his chin stuck out in determination, "before someone tries to stop me."

Ben would try to stop him, he felt, just as he had done before. The strong man would talk to him about running away when the going got tough. Still, he couldn't say that now. For Toby felt he was going *back* where things were tough. Anyway, he didn't want to listen to any of Ben's talk now.

He didn't want to talk to Sam either. It would be so hard to say good-by to the clown.

Colonel Castle wouldn't like his sudden leave taking. Not after all the weeks of training Toby had been given. It would take time to train a new rider to the peak of perfection Jeanette needed in a partner.

And Jeanette—Toby set his mouth in a grim line. He didn't want to talk or say good-by to *anybody*.

Uneasiness showed on Mr. Stubbs's wizened face. He scratched his ear frantically, and looked around as if in search of someone to help.

But there was no one near.

Ben was on the platform in the north ring under the big top. He was nearing the climax of his strong man act, the ponies going round and round on the ends of the bar across his mighty shoulders.

At the performers' entrance to the big top, Sam Treat was waiting for his cue to go on.

With a last pat for his beautiful costume Toby picked up his own clothes and hastily pulled them on. Without a backward glance he started for the door.

Once there, he came to a sudden stop. He looked back at Mr. Stubbs. It wasn't fair to leave his friends like this, he thought guiltily. Sneaking off, that was what he was really doing.

In spite of his hurry he went back into the tent. He dug around until he found the tablet and stub of a pencil that belonged to Sam Treat.

He wrote a note, trying his best to explain the message in the letter from Aunt Olive and why he had to leave the circus and go back home. He folded it and stuck it in the corner of the mirror of the dressing table.

He felt better.

Mr. Stubbs still sat, eying him apprehensively.

Toby, seeing the look on the chimp's face, tried to explain.

"It's for Ben and Sam," he said, waving a hand toward the note and adding, "They can say good-by to everyone for me."

Mr. Stubbs looked at him reproachfully. Toby walked over to where the chimp sat. He picked up Mr. Stubbs and hugged him tightly. Mr. Stubbs made little noises of affection in his throat.

Toby looked at Mr. Stubbs and pleaded for understanding. "Mr. Stubbs," his voice shook with the emotion that welled up inside him at sight of the doleful look on the chimp's face, "I can't take you with me."

Mr. Stubbs clung to him. Burying his face on Toby's chest he whimpered.

The lump in Toby's throat grew bigger and bigger. Now he knew who, of all his circus friends, it was hardest to leave. He loved Mr. Stubbs and Mr. Stubbs loved him. The chimp was the only creature Toby could remember who had ever openly showed love and affection for him.

He laid his cheek against Mr. Stubbs's head. "You don't belong to me, you know," he whispered into the chimp's big ear. "They'd say I stole you. You understand, don't you?"

Mr. Stubbs didn't answer.

"I'll come back and get you some day," Toby promised in desperation. "Honest, I will!"

He hugged the chimp again. Then he set him down on the ground and checked the tether to be sure it was tied securely. Toby didn't want Mr. Stubbs following him and getting lost.

Mr. Stubbs looked reproachfully up at him. Toby,

how could you do this to me, your best friend? the gaze seemed to ask. Toby looked the other way and walked hurriedly out of the tent.

Mr. Stubbs watched him go. For a moment he sat quietly where Toby had left him, as though trying to understand. But apparently the only thing he could understand was that his friend had left him and wasn't coming back.

Mr. Stubbs felt he had to do something. So he lifted his head and let out a cry that was almost human. Wait, the cry seemed to say, wait for me!

The chimp threw his weight against the tether and tried his best to break it. But it was strong rope and d not break easily.

Mr. Stubbs did not give up. All the while Toby was walking across the circus ground, Mr. Stubbs kept hurling himself against that tether.

Toby stopped at the edge of the grounds and turned for a last farewell look at the circus he had come to know and love so much.

As he did so the tether snapped and Mr. Stubbs was free. The chimp looked surprised as the broken end of the rope flipped back and almost hit him in the face.

But he recovered quickly. With a glad cry he loped out of the tent in search of Toby.

Soon Toby was out of the tiny hamlet in which the circus was playing and walking with purposeful strides along a country road. He had no way of knowing that Mr. Stubbs was out of the dressing tent and running through the circus grounds looking for him.

He could not know either that, shortly after Mr. Stubbs's departure, Harry Tupper had come into the tent hoping to find him there.

Mr. Tupper had come to congratulate Toby for his fine performance in the show that day. For, as Tupper had reasoned, it would pay to keep in the good graces of the boy and make him think he was his great and good friend.

Tupper looked around and saw the tent was empty. Now, where had that brat gone? He could be the most irritating—his eye fell on the note stuck in the corner of the mirror.

A cloud passed over the ferrety face of the concession-aire. Now what had happened?

Quickly he yanked the note from the edge of the frame around the mirror. Peering carefully around to

see that no one was watching, he unfolded the paper
and read Toby's farewell message to his two friends.

Tupper's face reddened with anger. This was a pretty
kettle of fish! If that kid weren't around to ride with
Jeanette the twenty dollars a week finding fee from
Colonel Castle would come to an end.

The full realization hit Harry Tupper like a ton of
bricks dumped on his head—and his pocketbook. After
all he had done for that brat!

Viciously he crushed the note into a ball. "That ungrateful little whelp!" he muttered, thrusting the note
into his pocket.

Now, where was that monk?

Turning to leave, Tupper saw the broken tether. Slowly
he walked over to it, picked up the broken end, and
examined it. A faint smile broke across his face. He
turned and hurried out, a plan already forming in his
crafty mind.

14   FALSE HOPES

It was early the next morning. A bright sun shimmered down through the trees along a country road, making spangled patterns on the grassy earth below.

Busy sounds were in the air, the lowing of a cow, dogs barking, the clatter of milk cans from a nearby farmhouse, and the banging of a screen door. From somewhere came the raucous crow of a rooster.

Beneath the spreading limbs of a big oak tree beside the road, Toby Tyler still slept. None of the sounds had yet penetrated his sleep-filled mind. He had been dog-tired when he stopped here, at dusk, the day before. He had no way of telling how many miles he had covered since he had left the grounds of Colonel Sam Castle's Great American Circus, but his legs had ached as though he had walked from coast to coast!

He had stopped just once, at a farmhouse, where he had asked for food. The farmer's wife had made two big sandwiches for him, from fresh bread she had just taken from the oven. She had given him all the milk he could drink. He had eaten the feast on her back porch, shaded by a spreading oak tree.

When he had eaten the last crumb of food and swallowed the last of the milk, he had offered to pay the motherly looking woman for the food and the trouble she had taken to prepare it. But she had firmly refused to take any of his money.

She had told him she often got lonely for someone to talk to, that it was a real treat to welcome someone from so interesting a place as a circus. She had really been awed when he told her he had ridden in the equestrian act in the big show. She said it seemed a shame to have to give up such a wonderful career. But when he had told her where he was going and why, she had agreed he was doing the right thing.

After leaving the nice lady he had walked several miles farther. He had found this sheltered spot beneath the tree where he had lain down and gone to sleep.

As the rays of the sun filtered through the leaves of

the tree and warmed the back of his neck, Toby stirred a little. He rolled over into a more comfortable position. But he did not waken.

Suddenly he sat up, startled. Something had hit him on the end of his freckled nose. The sting brought with it a this-has-happened-to-me-before feeling. He looked up and his eyes popped.

There, sitting on a branch just above him, was Mr. Stubbs, chattering happily!

"Mr. Stubbs!" Toby cried in wide-eyed surprise.

The chimp gave him a toothy grin. Then, with great agility, he jumped down from his perch and hopped gleefully up and down in front of Toby.

Misgivings piled up within Toby. Mr. Stubbs should not be here with him on this country road. The chimp belonged to Colonel Castle and should be with the circus. But he was Toby's friend, too, the most loving, affectionate creature Toby had ever known, and Toby was happy to see him.

Toby leaned over and picked up Mr. Stubbs. He hugged the chimp, hard. Mr. Stubbs puckered up and planted a big kiss on Toby's cheek.

Toby felt guilty in spite of himself.

"What are you doing here?" he asked of Mr. Stubbs, at the same time giving the chimp another squeeze. "They'll be after me for sure now. Gosh, Mr. Stubbs!"

Though anxiety furrowed his boyish brow he decided to enjoy the company of Mr. Stubbs as long as he could. After all, he couldn't turn the chimp around and tell him to go back where he had come from, could he? The chimp wouldn't know the way and wouldn't take it if he did. Toby's conscience did a fast retreat.

Toby lifted Mr. Stubbs and set him on his shoulder. Together they headed across the dusty, weed-grown space between the tree and the road.

Toby grinned cheerfully as Mr. Stubbs chattered away.

"Well," Toby told his pal, shrugging his shoulder and jiggling Mr. Stubbs a bit, "the only thing I can do now is take you home with me. We'll write Colonel Castle and tell him where you are."

Mr. Stubbs chattered something like he thought it was a great idea. With steps as light as thistledown Toby moved off down the road singing "Beedle Dee I."

Harry Tupper wasn't in quite so merry a mood that morning as he pulled up in front of a country store. He leaped out of the rented rig he had been driving at

a fast pace since he had left the little town in which the circus was playing. Into the store he raced.

It was a general store and like others of the day carried everything from boots to buggy whips. It smelled of dill pickles lying in frothy brine in a barrel in a corner, and dried apples in a wooden crate, and well-oiled leather. In a glass-enclosed showcase on one side of the long, narrow building were rows and rows of coconut drop candy, pink and white and green, and red-and-white striped peppermint sticks.

Behind the showcase were shelves of brightly colored bolts of calico and gingham, and across the way were more shelves full of canned goods and boxes. In between, piled every which way on the floor, were boxes and barrels and cartons.

In one corner Jim Weaver was buying some cartridges for the time-worn Winchester rifle that leaned against the counter beside him. Waiting patiently beside the young hunter was his handsome dog.

Harry Tupper dashed up beside Weaver.

"Morning, gentlemen!" he said brusquely.

The proprietor lifted his head. One hand still on the box of cartridges, he answered briefly, "Day."

It was easy to see he thought Tupper lacking in manners when he interrupted him while he was waiting on another customer.

That did not bother Tupper.

"Got a phone?" he demanded.

Over the rims of his old-fashioned spectacles the proprietor of the store flashed him a look of annoyance. He gave a curt nod toward the telephone hanging on the wall at the end of the store. Then he went back to counting out the cartridges Weaver had bought.

Tupper strode toward the telephone. Picking up the receiver he whirled the crank on the side of the instrument. Half turning, his cold gray eyes swept the interior of the store in the contemptuous manner of one accustomed to trading in much better places.

If the proprietor of the store and young Weaver saw the look, they gave no sign of it. They went right on with their business, ignoring the brash newcomer.

Tupper did not like that. He would soon show these yokels what an important man he was.

His eyes still on the men at the counter, he said loudly into the mouthpiece, "Operator! Get me the sheriff over to Bartonsville. It's important."

Tupper was sure then that the proprietor and the hunter tensed slightly. Now they wanted to hear what he had to say. The owner of the store even looked up at him, briefly, before taking a bill from his customer and ringing up the sale on the cash register.

Tupper made the matter sound even more urgent.

"Sheriff?" he asked importantly. "This is Harry Tupper, representing Castle's Great American Circus." There was a pause. "Yes. . . ."

Tupper added as much drama to what he had to say as he could. The men had their backs to him, yet he knew they were listening.

"I want you to look out for a small boy about eleven years old, calls himself Toby Tyler. I figure he's goin' in your direction—"

Tupper paused then, impatiently listening to something the sheriff said. Eying the ceiling he tapped on the arm of the mouthpiece with a long finger.

At the first break he resumed his own recital.

"He ran away from the circus last night," he said with exaggerated gravity. "Took along a valuable animal belonging to Colonel Castle. A chimpanzee."

Deliberately the proprietor counted change into young

Weaver's hand. At the same time they exchanged meaningful glances. Tupper, watchful eyes on them, knew he was making an impression.

Tupper lowered his voice to a just-between-you-and-me tone.

"Thanks, Sheriff," he said. "You find him, we'll be glad to express our appreciation, if you know what I mean."

Hanging up the receiver, he turned toward Weaver and the proprietor. Swaggering, he walked over to where they stood.

He twirled his straw hat around one finger and looked over some stock with the attitude of one who could buy out the place if he wished.

"Don't suppose either of you have glimpsed the lad?" he asked with studied unconcern.

The proprietor gave Tupper a long, slow look and shook his head. He had seen a good many of this kind in his day and had never liked them. Big talk they were full of, with little to back it up.

Didn't get much out of him, Tupper thought. He turned to the young hunter. Better use a different approach, he reasoned. Sometimes these hicks were touchy.

He smiled in his most ingratiating manner. A little buttering up was all this young Daniel Boone needed.

"You probably know this part of the country pretty well," he said flatteringly. "You find this boy, there's a reward of—uh—ten dollars in it for you."

Jim Weaver's lip curled. His honest blue eyes swept the concessionaire from the top of his thinning hair to the pointed tips of his dusty shoes. He replied in a voice sharp with contempt, "Sorry, I'm not much at trackin' small boys. Bobcats is about fearsome enough for me."

Tupper was taken aback. He had been so sure this hayseed would do anything for ten dollars! But he managed to shrug and say, "Suit yourself." Then he hastened out of the store.

The eyes of Weaver and the store owner followed him with distaste. They stayed on him until he had climbed into his rented spring wagon, and with a flourish of the reins, driven away.

Tupper did not know that, not far down the road, Toby stood behind a tree and watched him go by.

Toby's eyes followed the wagon until it had disappeared around a bend in the road. He listened until the rattle could no longer be heard. Then, and only then, he turned to Mr. Stubbs and said, "We'll cut across here."

With Mr. Stubbs hopping along beside him, he turned and plunged deeper into the woods. From now on he would keep away from roads if he could.

The woods thinned out into a softly rolling knoll. Toby and Mr. Stubbs crossed the clearing slowly. Toby was winded from that run away from the road. Once across the knoll Mr. Stubbs scampered on well ahead of Toby. Toby saw the chimp disappear into the undergrowth. Alarm rose within him.

"Mr. Stubbs!" he cried. "Not so fast! *Wait* for me!"

Harry Tupper heard the cry come faintly from the woods. He stopped the wagon, stood up, and looked into the thicket beside the road. He listened intently. Was that the kid's voice, he wondered.

In the same woods Jim Weaver was following a familiar, well-worn path, his dog running and sniffing at his side. Suddenly the dog stopped, his ears going up.

"You raisin' something, Mary?" Weaver asked.

The dog yelped and lit out into the brush. Weaver followed, his gun held in readiness.

Toby could not see Mr. Stubbs. But he could hear the chimp chattering. Following the sound as best he could, Toby cried out several times, "Mr. Stubbs! Where are you? Mr Stubbs!"

Mr. Stubbs paid no attention to Toby. He kept right on scooting along on the ground, chattering away at nothing in particular. Then, suddenly, he heard the barking of a nearby dog. As the dog drew closer, Mr. Stubbs streaked off to what he thought was the safety of the underbrush.

Toby kept right on following the chattering sound. He hoped he would find Mr. Stubbs soon. When he did, he wouldn't let loose of him until they were out of this woods.

Jim Weaver followed the excited barking of his dog. Harry Tupper stood in his wagon, listening to the baying and wondering what was going on in there in the woods.

Suddenly Mr. Stubbs found himself in a small clearing. Frightened now by the closeness of the barking, the chimp raced across the grassy spot and headed up a tree on the other side.

The dog and Jim Weaver appeared in the clearing

then. The dog ran to the base of the tree up which the chimp had climbed, and looking up, barked louder than ever.

Weaver looked up too. He could see the leaves of the tree moving. The dog had treed something all right. Weaver raised his rifle.

"Mr. Stubbs!" Toby was calling not far away. "Where are you?"

Like thunder in his ears he heard the crack of the rifle. Cold terror clutched at him. Panic-stricken, he ran in the direction from which the sound had come.

"Mr. Stubbs!" he wailed heartbrokenly. *"Mr. Stubbs!"*

Tupper heard the shot too. He jumped down from the wagon and plunged into the woods.

Toby reached the clearing just in time to hear something crash through the branches above his head. To his utter horror the form of Mr. Stubbs tumbled down through the leaves and thudded to the ground a few feet away!

Toby could see the blood gushing from the wound in the chimp's chest. He stood as though paralyzed, unable to believe what he saw.

A few minutes ago his little pal had been scampering

along beside him. Now he lay on the ground, making no motion and no sound. That couldn't have happened to Mr. Stubbs! Toby knew he would wake up soon and find it had been a bad dream.

But he *was* awake, and there was Mr. Stubbs shot by a heartless hunter. A wave of anguish swept over Toby, leaving him weak and trembling.

Uttering a grief-stricken cry, the boy ran to the side of the chimpanzee and dropped to his knees.

"Mr. Stubbs! Oh, Mr. Stubbs!" he moaned.

Mr. Stubbs gave him no mischievous look. His eyes were shut. There was no mocking grin. The lips remained closed.

Tenderly Toby took the small form in his arms and gently rocked back and forth. He picked up one of the small paws.

"Mr. Stubbs, don't! Don't leave me!"

Jim Weaver stood at the edge of the clearing. He watched the boy race to the side of the animal he had shot. He knew at once what he had done. A feeling of remorse engulfed him.

He had been a boy once. A dog of his had been accidentally killed. How well he remembered the grief he had felt then. He knew too well that nothing he could say or do would lessen the sorrow of the boy kneeling there beneath the tree with the animal in his arms.

Something had told Weaver, the instant he pulled the trigger, that the animal he had shot was not an ordinary woodland animal, like a squirrel. The heavy crash of the body tumbling from the tree had made him certain of it. What kind of an animal was it? Only a few animals of the region lived in trees—squirrels, possums, and such. It couldn't be one of those.

But a chimpanzee! He remembered, then, the man at the store who had telephoned the sheriff.

"He ran away from the circus last night," the man had said. "Took along a valuable animal belonging to Colonel Castle. A chimpanzee."

Where but at a circus or a zoo would one find a chimpanzee? This was the boy the man had spoken of, Weaver was certain of it. The young hunter felt sorrier than ever for the lad, and his burden of remorse became heavier.

With heavy steps he walked over to where Toby Tyler rocked back and forth on his knees, the still form of Mr. Stubbs in his arms. He looked down at the boy, deep sympathy on his face. He started to speak, but no words would come.

Toby sensed someone near him. He looked up and saw the gun and knew.

"You did it!" Toby cried, tears streaming down his face. "You shot him! Why? Why?"

Weaver struggled for an answer.

"I had no idea that—" he stammered. "I thought it was—"

He stepped forward, hand outstretched. His heart was full of compassion for the boy. He wanted to do something, say something.

Toby turned on him with the ferocity of the mother of a wounded cub.

"You killed him!" Toby cried bitterly. "You're a murderer."

Weaver drew back his hand and flexed his fingers to relieve the tension. His strong rugged features were creased with concern.

"Believe me," he said softly. "I'm sorry."

His words had no effect on Toby but to deepen his sorrow.

"You killed the only one I ever had to love me!" the boy sobbed.

Weaver laid down his gun. It would be a long time before he used it again. He tried to lay his hand on Toby's shaking shoulders. But Toby jerked fiercely away.

"Go away!" Toby cried. "Get away from us!"

He buried his face in Mr. Stubbs's neck and sobbed heartbreakingly.

Weaver stood silently looking down at the boy, sick with the knowledge of what he had done and the futility of trying to undo it.

Neither Weaver nor Toby saw Harry Tupper reach the edge of the clearing and stand looking at the scene before him. Silent for a second, the concessionaire stepped up to where Toby mourned his little friend.

"What's this?" he asked sharply. "What happened?"

Toby looked up, knowing who it was. Coldly he turned away from both men who would rob him of the one he held most dear.

In Tupper there was no compassion. He simply said, "That's too bad, Toby! That's really too bad."

The concessionaire bent over Toby and tried to pull him to his feet.

"You see, Toby?" he said without a flicker of sympathy in voice or manner. "If you hadn't run away this terrible thing wouldn't have happened." He paused for a moment to let his accusation sink in and take effect. "It's your fault."

Toby looked down at Mr. Stubbs, tears flowing down his cheeks.

"My fault?" he whispered, stricken suddenly with the terrible realization that it *had* been he who had failed to return Mr. Stubbs to the circus that morning. If he had done so, Mr. Stubbs would not have been in these woods, would not be . . . . Toby looked down at Mr. Stubbs and sobbed harder than ever.

Tupper callously continued to rub salt into Toby's already wounded conscience by continuing, "Surely you see that, don't you? Mr. Stubbs would be alive and well now if you hadn't run off. Come now, let's go back. Maybe the colonel will give you another pet."

Toby fought wildly. "I want Mr. Stubbs!"

Of all the stubborn brats, Tupper thought, this one took the cake. He was enough to tax the patience of the kindest man. Besides, he had to get him back to the circus somehow or lose that twenty dollars a week.

Tupper's already thin patience snapped. "Don't be stupid!" he said angrily. "Mr. Stubbs is dead. There's nothing you can do to change that. Come on, now."

Tupper reached over and grabbed Toby again by the collar of his jacket. He pulled at the boy. Toby resisted, harder than ever.

"Mr. Stubbs! No! I won't leave him!"

Tupper put all his strength into the effort and yanked hard. In spite of himself Toby was pulled to his feet. As he did so his hold on Mr. Stubbs was loosened and the little chimp's body rolled to the ground.

Toby tried to pick up his pal again, but Tupper kept a firm grip on him and forcibly led him away.

Weaver watched the whole thing, his sympathy for Toby growing by the second. He felt he had to do something.

"It's not the boy's fault," he protested to Tupper. "It's mine."

Tupper halted his march toward the road. He turned and said magnanimously, "Forget it, young fellow. Accidents will happen. The important thing is, we found the lad safe and sound."

Weaver realized there was nothing he could do for

the boy. But he did feel sorry for him as he stood and watched Tupper pull and yank him, sobbing, back toward the wagon.

A few minutes later Tupper jerked Toby into the rig. Then he jumped in himself and drove away.

Weaver stood silently for a minute after Toby and Tupper disappeared into the woods between the clearing and the road. Then he walked back to the spot where they had left the body of the little chimp. He would bury it. That was the least he could do now.

He reached the spot and looked, his eyes popping. The chimp wasn't there! Hastily he looked around. Not a sign of Mr. Stubbs could he see.

Suddenly elated he picked up his rifle and started to run toward the road. He would tell the boy the good news. The chimp couldn't have been so badly hurt if he had gotten up and walked away!

"Hey! Wait!" Weaver yelled, hoping Tupper and the boy would hear him. But he received no answer.

Weaver kept on running. He reached the road and was just in time to see the rig disappearing in a cloud of dust.

Perhaps it was just as well he had not raised false

hopes in the boy. The chimp might have crawled off to die alone. Animals often did that.

"C'mon, girl!" he called to his dog. "Let's find him!"

Weaver and the dog went back into the woods. If the chimp were really dead it would be best to leave things as they were.

15 OUR BOY!

Toby sat numbly on the seat beside Harry Tupper. As the wagon bounced along the bumpy country road, he looked the picture of abject misery.

He was going back to the circus. In a way he should be glad of that. But the circus wouldn't be the same now, not with Mr. Stubbs gone. It had been his fault! If only he hadn't . . . if, if, if!

Neither Toby nor Tupper said a word to each other on the long trip back.

The circus lot was quiet as they drove into it. Harry headed the rig straight toward Colonel Castle's white office wagon.

At the sight of the owner's wagon Toby came to sudden life. He sprang off the seat and ran toward the office of Colonel Castle.

Toby's action took Tupper by complete surprise. At the same time the concessionaire became alarmed. It might not be to his best interests for Toby to get to Colonel Castle first. You had no way of knowing what a kid might blab.

"Just a minute!" Tupper cried. "I'll tell him! Stop!"

Tupper jumped out of the wagon and took off after Toby. But he was too late. Toby had dashed up the steps of Castle's wagon and burst into the door before Tupper could reach him.

Colonel Castle was seated at his desk at the end of the wagon. Toby ran up to him. In his haste Toby did not see the other two people seated there.

"Colonel Castle!" he cried breathlessly. "It was my fault! I ran away and Mr. Stubbs ran after me! I didn't want it to happen!"

Colonel Castle gave Toby a gentle smile.

"Toby," he said softly, "there's someone here to see you."

Toby whirled. He froze. There, in chairs alongside the colonel's desk, sat Aunt Olive and Uncle Daniel!

For a fleeting second Toby stood and stared. Then, with a glad cry, he fled into the outstretched arms of

Aunt Olive and buried his face on her shoulder.

He hugged Aunt Olive as hard as he could and she kissed him fondly. Oh, what a comfort were her arms! There he could forget the hurts of the morning—almost.

For several wordless seconds Toby and Aunt Olive clung to each other. Then Toby looked up into the eyes of Uncle Daniel.

Uncle Daniel's jaw muscles were working the same as Ben's did when he was trying to hide the feelings he had inside. Ben had taught Toby a lot of things and one of them was that men never wanted to show emotions, especially of the sentimental kind.

Aunt Olive relaxed her hold on Toby. Slowly he started toward Uncle Daniel, trying to figure out what the old man's reactions would be. Uncle Daniel saw the boy's hesitancy, and knowing the reason for it, held out his arms. Happily, Toby ran into them.

The old man hugged him as hard as Aunt Olive had. Toby hugged Uncle Daniel right back, his smooth young cheek held close against the rough old one. Uncle Daniel asked chokingly, "Toby! Will you forgive me?"

His ears alert for any sound from within, Harry Tupper stood by the door of the wagon. He heard

Uncle Daniel's remark, and peering around and into the wagon, he saw Toby in Uncle Daniel's arms.

The concessionaire didn't like what he saw and heard. But before he had a chance to think what he was going to do about it, a huge hand lifted him up and off the steps.

There was Ben Cotter. The face of the strong man was grim and forbidding as he held Tupper up very close.

"You lily-livered skunk!" Ben snarled into Harry Tupper's ear. "I found out what you did with Toby's letters!"

The whites of Tupper's eyes widened as he grimaced in terror.

"Ben! Don't!" he cried.

Fiercely Ben glowered at him, shaking him until his teeth rattled.

"Tampering with the mails," Ben gritted, "that calls for a jail sentence, Mr. Tupper!"

Tupper whimpered, "Ben, you're hurting me!"

Ben snorted contemptuously. "I'll make you one of those gentlemen's agreements you're so fond of, Mr. Tupper. I want you to give up that share of Toby's money that you've been getting."

"I will, Ben!" Tupper wailed piteously. "I will!"

With effortless ease, Ben then carried the concessionaire toward a nearby tub of water.

As he went, he kept on in the same grim tone, "I want you to stay away from that boy. I want you to behave nice and pretty. Because if you don't, I'm liable to do something like this."

For a second Ben held Tupper over the water and then, disdainfully, he let him drop. Tupper hit the water with a loud splash. He went under and came up sputtering. When he did, Ben casually reached over and snatched a towel from around the neck of a grinning roustabout and tossed it to Tupper.

It was an hour or so before the evening performance. Toby, wearing a robe over his splendid riding costume, was showing Aunt Olive and Uncle Ben around the circus grounds. He was as happy as was possible without having Mr. Stubbs around.

Signorina Zorelda passed them and gave Toby a lovely smile.

"Happy to see you back, Toby," she said.

Toby smiled shyly. "Thank you," he answered.

Two clowns went by. They waved at the boy showing the old folks around.

"Looks like a full house tonight, Toby," one of them said jovially. "Knock 'em dead."

"Sure," Toby answered right back.

Toby and Aunt Olive and Uncle Daniel neared the monkey wagon. At sight of it Toby's happiness took sudden leave. He felt empty and miserable. Mr. Stubbs! Oh, how he wished Mr. Stubbs were in that cage right now, throwing twigs at him, swiping his candy apple, or just grinning impishly at him! The thought of the chimp alone out there in the woods was almost more than Toby could bear. His lip trembled and his eyes saddened.

"You've made a lot of good friends, Toby," Uncle Daniel said gently.

Toby looked up at his uncle. He was grateful to his folks for having come right at this time. They helped make his grief a little more bearable. Toby sighed deeply.

"I just wish you could have met Mr. Stubbs," he said wistfully.

He forced himself to look into the wagon. Its emptiness hit him an almost physical blow. He didn't see Ben come up.

"This was his wagon," Toby went on and his voice trembled with emotion. "He was my best friend of all."

Then he turned away. He just couldn't talk about Mr. Stubbs anymore.

Ben interrupted. "Toby—sorry to bother you. Can you run over and tell Sam Treat to meet me at the stock tent? Right away?"

"Sure," Toby answered, glad for the chance to get away from that cage and the memories it brought back to him so forcefully.

Ben watched Toby leave. Then he turned toward Aunt Olive and Uncle Daniel and gave them a friendly, welcoming grin.

Toby headed for Sam Treat's tent. He hurried through the entrance flap and stopped short. There, standing inside the tent with his dog beside him, was Jim Weaver, the man who had shot Mr. Stubbs!

"You!" grated Toby. "What are you doing here?"

Weaver grinned maddeningly at Toby. He stepped to one side. As he did so, his dog's tail began to wave— joyously, it seemed to Toby. Of all the nerve! What did they have to be so happy about? But, then, Mr. Stubbs hadn't meant anything to *them*.

Toby stared between them. Something was going on at the table beyond. Sam Treat's dogs were gathered around it, intently looking down at something on it. Their tails were wagging joyously too!

Then, from the midst of the waggle-tail dogs, Toby heard a familiar sound. Oh, no! It couldn't be! With one leap he had reached the side of the table. He looked over the dogs and gave a wild cry of joy. There lay Mr. Stubbs!

The chimp's chest was swathed in bandages, but his eyes were open and the old mischievous twinkle was there, undimmed.

"Mr. Stubbs!" Toby could have been heard above the trumpet of an elephant. "Oh, Mr. Stubbs!"

Then suddenly he whirled and looked at Sam Treat. His blue eyes had clouded over with doubt.

"Is he all right?" he asked with bated breath.

Sam nodded.

"Bullet just ventilated his hide a little," the clown smiled. "Remember what I said? You can't kill the chimp." Sam struggled for a word. "He's indestruct—

indestric—indes— you couldn't do it!"

Toby grinned then and relaxed. He hugged Mr. Stubbs to him, hard.

Later that evening the show was in full swing. At the performers' entrance to the big top, Toby and Jeanette waited for their cue to go on. Toby's happiness was complete. Mr. Stubbs was back and Aunt Olive and Uncle Daniel were there in the audience. All that remained for him to do now was to put on a crackajack of a performance for them.

A roll of drums sounded. Toby and Jeanette smiled reassuringly at each other. Toby knew now that, no matter how many times he would go into that tent to perform, he would always have a touch of stage fright at the entrance.

Colonel Castle's voice came to them. "Ladies and gentlemen! For your kind approval—*Mademoiselle* Jeanette and *Monsieur* Toby, world famous young equestrians in feats of grace and daring!"

Another roll of drums sounded. Toby and Jeanette, standing on the backs of their resin backs, trotted into the arena. They were so handsome and so graceful and so young! The crowd applauded enthusiastically.

Jeanette and Toby bowed.

Toby remembered something then and trembled a little. Just before the show Colonel Castle had come to him and asked if he would like to do his new trick for tonight's show. Toby had been practicing it for quite a while and thought, at the time, that it would be nice to do it for the special benefit of Aunt Olive and Uncle Daniel. He had told Colonel Castle that he would.

Now he was beginning to wonder if it had been such a good idea. Suppose he made some silly blunder? Perhaps he should have stuck to the routine he was sure he could do right.

But it was too late now to change his mind.

He looked for Aunt Olive and Uncle Daniel, seated, he knew, somewhere out there in the audience. Then he saw them in a front row applauding mightily.

He could not fail them tonight. He would do that new routine perfectly or know the reason why.

A performer had to feel good, mentally and physically, to give a good account of himself in the ring. Toby felt fine, now that Mr. Stubbs was back and tethered in the dressing tent.

Toby saw the tousle-headed boy who had taken his place at the lemonade stand. The boy was standing in an aisle, eyes wide and mouth agape, watching Toby.

Toby grinned and bowed in the boy's direction. He knew exactly how that boy felt. He had felt the same way not so long ago when he carried the tray and stood looking at Jeanette and Ajax.

He saw Harry Tupper appear then, too, and poke the new boy roughly. The boy then took off up an aisle, crying his wares. Toby knew how that felt too.

He saw Ben in his strong man's costume give Tupper a stern look. Good old Ben! He was going to look after that boy as well.

The music of the act went on, and on, and on. Mr. Stubbs stood it as long as he could. Then he tried to do something about that tether. He had broken it once before, so why couldn't he do it again? He began to work furiously at it.

Toby and Jeanette were going on with their act, unaware of Mr. Stubbs's chagrin. They jumped over the obstacles while the audience gasped and applauded,

Aunt Olive and Uncle Daniel louder than anybody.

Sam and Colonel Castle watched the two youngsters go through their paces. The faces of both men glowed with pride and satisfaction.

Again Colonel Castle stepped into the center of the ring. He raised his hand as a signal for the applause to stop. Then he said, "Now, ladies and gentlemen, may I direct your attention to a feat of balance and horsemanship seldom witnessed in the sawdust ring! Are you ready, *Monsieur* Toby?"

This is it, thought Toby. He crossed his fingers and gave the "ready" signal. Castle waved to the leader of the band, and the music for the new stunt began.

Just as Toby trotted around the ring to begin his stunt, a tiny part of the bottom edge of the tent wall lifted and Mr. Stubbs peered into the big top. Seeing nothing to stop him, the chimp scampered under the seats toward the ring, where he knew his pal Toby was performing.

As his horse trotted slowly around, Toby took a kitchen chair handed to him by a roustabout. He fitted it into a special rig on the horse's back. Placed just right, the rig held the chair up on its two hind legs.

When he had the legs of the chair settled to his satisfaction, Toby sat down in the seat. He balanced himself there right handily. So far, so good. The applause came to him in waves.

It was Ben who saw Mr. Stubbs come out from under the seats and head for the ring. The strong man knew the chimp was up to no good.

Ben tried to head off Mr. Stubbs. But the chimp was adept at dodging and quickly eluded the big man.

Mr. Stubbs reached the edge of the ring. He scampered around it until he came abreast of Toby and his horse. Then he gave a flying leap and landed on the rear flank of Toby's mount!

Toby saw him coming and closed his eyes and—the next thing he knew Mr. Stubbs was on one of his shoulders! The chair teetered precariously. With a mighty effort Toby righted it.

"Mr. Stubbs!" he cried in real alarm. "Look out!"

Mr. Stubbs obliged by clutching him around the neck and showing him how much love he had in his chimpanzee heart for his friend. The horse kept right on cantering around the ring.

Aunt Olive and Uncle Daniel, sitting nearby, thought

it was very funny. They laughed and clapped and so did the rest of the audience.

Toby gritted his teeth and hoped for the best. There wasn't anything else he could do!

There was plenty more that Mr. Stubbs could do, and he promptly proceeded to do it. He clamped his paws around Toby's eyes so Toby couldn't see a thing!

"Mr. Stubbs!" Toby pleaded. "Cut it out!"

Colonel Castle and Sam watched intently. What was going to happen next? Ben, alarmed, came up to them.

"Sorry about this, Colonel," the big man said apologetically, "I tried to nail him, but he got away from me."

His voice trailed off. He was watching the expression on Colonel Castle's face. It was not the look of exasperation that he had expected.

Instead Colonel Castle jerked a thumb toward the audience. The folks were laughing and enjoying themselves hugely.

Castle looked at Ben.

"Ben," he said thoughtfully, "I got an idea!"

Ben, pleased that the colonel wasn't angry at what he thought had been a slip on his part, said quickly,

"Sure, Colonel. You just tell me what—"

Then a terrible thought broke on Ben. He held up one hand in horror.

"No, Colonel! No!"

Castle nodded, pleased with himself.

"Ben," he said firmly, "I want you to teach that chimp how to ride. Work him into the act."

Ben was adamant. Scowling fiercely, he growled, "No, sir! Me work with that thieving, conniving, ornery trouble-making little. . . . *No, Sir!*"

Ben made the last "No, sir" as final as his big voice could make it.

Colonel Castle seemed to look right through him.

"Great, isn't he?" he said enthusiastically. "We'll bill him as *Monsieur* Stubbs!"

The colonel walked away on cloud nine.

Sam looked at Ben and started to say something. But he thought better of it and made ready to leave, only to find he couldn't. Ben's big foot was planted firmly on his own!

Ben said resignedly, "*Monsieur* Stubbs!"

Sam added sadly, "Heh, heh! Sure!"

The act was over. Toby rose from the chair, turned

and picked it up. He dropped it into the hands of a waiting roustabout. Then he disengaged Mr. Stubbs from around his neck and held him high up in the air over his head.

The crowd went wild.

Toby was thinking he would try to talk Colonel Castle into letting Mr. Stubbs become a regular part of the act. It would be easy to teach the chimp to leap onto the back of the horse more carefully so as not to upset him and the chair.

Just look at all the applause the chimp was getting.

Aunt Olive and Uncle Daniel were standing up and applauding. They both heard a woman nearby say to her husband, "Isn't he wonderful?"

Toby and Jeanette jumped through the flaming hoop. They leaped down from their horses, and each holding a paw of Mr. Stubbs, they took another bow.

Uncle Daniel could stand it no longer. He turned to the woman who had expressed her admiration for Toby and said proudly, "He's *our* boy!"